Find out more about this author and upcoming book at her website, lsengler.com, or follow her on Twitter @lsengler

THE SLAYER SAGA:

SOULLESS

PROLOGUE

She would never forget the day the world changed.

The grotesque scenes were still so vivid in her mind whenever she heard the crackle of a fire in the village square, rich with the smoky scent of sap and ashes. It took her back to a time when she was still a little girl, wrapped in a thick woolen blanket and sitting on her mother's lap. Her wide eyes reflected the dancing flames as she stared at the myth teller, captivated by his words. He was such a fascinating figure; not even his age could mar his graceful moments and his lively voice. He wore a long silk cloak, spreading out behind him like evening covering a painted sunset sky. The bones in his long grey hair rattled in accompaniment to his slow, gripping story. The little girl squirmed as she listened, burying herself deeper into her mother's embrace.

"Like a dark cloud bringing ruinous rains," the myth teller said, "the plight of the Soulless sweeps over the land and covers it in darkness. Some may find refuge in time, but most are washed away in the deluge. It is not a cleansing bath. The merciless waters take much, but they leave behind even more, all the sludge and slime and sediment of the terrible things they carried. Like a great smudge, they stain the world with a great evil, so deep it may never be cleaned. But even the heaviest of storms drain themselves out, and a light eventually penetrates through the thick gloom. So it is with the terror of the Soulless. The light comes in the form of a great warrior, a Savior to all Untouched. This hero will be merciless and cold, but great and powerful. By the stroke of the warrior's shining blade, the world will be restored to a peace known only by our ancestor's ancestor's ancestors. It is a peace that will not be known again until our children's children's children."

Even the rattling bones went quiet and still for the dramatic moment before the questions began. They were always the same questions, every retelling, but that first voice always wavered with uncertainty, emerging from a timid volunteer in the crowd.

"How will we know the hero," the shaking voice inquired, "when the hero comes?"

"The hero," said the myth teller, "will be unmistakable, armored in the light of righteousness, armed with the steel of justice. On the hero's crown, a helm of clarity and truth. On the hero's feet, great boots of grounding. All who look upon this strong warrior will feel awe; all Soulless will cower back in fear, for even those without Hearts will know their end is imminent from such a figure. There will be no mistaking the hero when the hero arrives, and there will be no hope to prepare for such a being."

"When," ventured the next voice, "will the hero come?"

"Our Savior" the myth teller said, "has no concept of time; the hero will appear only at the hour of our greatest need. No sooner. No later. We must be patient and hope that the hero comes for us, but we must understand, should this warrior not arrive, then it is not yet our darkest hour, however grim it may seem."

Before the next question could be asked, though, the little girl had grown restless with the story. She felt possessed with a sudden desire to change it, though it hadn't been changed for as long as anyone could remember.

"I want to be the Savior of the Untouched," she said, lifting her voice as high and loud as her small lungs could manage. Behind her, the little girl's mother drew in a sharp, terrified breath, as a stupefied silence settled over the villagers. It was as if she had taken time and held it still in her tiny hand. They could have never imagined anyone deviating from the legendary tale, least of all a child barely as tall as their hips. All eyes slowly turned toward the myth teller, seeking his ageless wisdom in this momentous event.

The old man set the end of his staff down into the dusty ground; the beads on the end clattered together like teeth. He leaned forward, peering at the little girl though his eyes were milky with blindness. She was tempted to draw back in remorseful penance for what she had done, but she refused to be ashamed. She had spoken the truth. She had given a voice to her heart's desire, and she knew the timing had been exactly right.

"Silly girl," said the myth teller, shaking his head as he chuckled, deep and rumbling. "A hero does not simply stand up and proclaim, 'I am a hero' and it is so. A hero is made, not through words, but through actions."

"Then I will act the hero," said the little girl, "and it will be so."

When the myth teller laughed at this, a few uncertain titters and smiles rose from the crowd, as if the old man's laughter was the permission they needed to be amused by the absurd scene. The tension in the air seemed to fade, if only slightly, as he reached out and gave the little girl a few soft pats on the top of her head with this thin hand of gnarled bone.

"I fear the golden armor of the Savior is too large for such a small person," he said. He turned away, back toward the fire, opening his arms in a grand gesture, as if he had barely missed a beat of his tale. "But perhaps the girl is right, and she will be our hero. Perhaps her youthful body will one day fit the golden armor after all; perhaps one day, instead of grasping at her mother's skirt, she will grasp the hilt of a sword. Only time will truly tell. Only in our time of great need--"

But the myth teller's tale was interrupted again, this time by the sudden, haunting horns from the watchtowers. The low, eerie sound reverberated through the air and sunk deep beneath the skin, holding them all with the tight grip of dread.

When the mournful horns filled the air for the second time, the peace of the evening shattered into a thousand glittering shards of chaos. The villagers scrambled, screaming in panic, moaning in fear. Women grabbed their children and fled for shelter. Men and boys went to gather their weapons.

Soulless had arrived, and death was not far behind.

The awful creatures emerged from the dark shadows of the night. Once, they may have been human, but that was a long time ago.   Now, their figures were distorted and putrefied, revealing their unnatural forms, so much like theirs once, before the rot grey and green rot of the virus changed them.   With their incredible strength, borne from some unknown demonic source, they mercilessly maimed anything unfortunate enough to cross their path, consuming their flesh and bone to feed an insatiable hunger. A fleeing mother's feet could not move her fast enough; a grey Soulless lunged for her legs, biting into the soft, tender flesh of her calf. As she fell, her child tumbled out of the safety of her arms.   Her wrenching scream intensified as she was forced to witness the creatures descend on the babe like ravenous dogs, a sight far more painful than the sharp teeth tearing into her from behind.

The carnage bred a multitude of horrific scenes.   A young man, breathless and bloody, managed to smash the head of a Soulless grasping his leg, only to turn and find a Soulless ready to crush his. A young boy barely lifted a spear before he burst open from the center, a gnarled and twisting hand reaching through him to get to the tender organs inside. The old myth teller himself was grabbed by the long braids of his hair, ripped clean from his scalp in one sharp movement. They smashed his head against a rock to expose the sweet grey matter within, slurping it up like soup. A young woman struggled with a Soulless at each of her arms, pulling and fighting and pulling some more until finally they tore her apart, her scream cut short as her bones popped and her flesh ripped.

Chaos, screaming, blood everywhere. The crackling fire now cast its light on an orgy of destruction. The blaze grew as people threw themselves in, preferring to be consumed by the flames than by the Soulless. The Soulless themselves leaped in after them, not willing to let their prey go so easily. Though their skin boiled and bubbled away, they found the strength to keep moving through the heat, unstoppable. They ignited into moving torches, catching fire to the thatched roofs and long, dry grass.

The little girl watched it all from the shelter of an old, broken cart, cast in heavy shadows. Her mother trembled over her and tried not to breath, tried not to cry, but the little girl felt the hot tears drip down on the top of her head. She could taste copper on her tongue, and the air was filled with a thick smokiness, putrid with the scent of burning flesh. Her stomach lurched, but she kept still. She kept her mouth shut and her eyes wide open.

Eventually, terror shook the little girl's mother so powerfully that it dislodged the last remaining bits of courage inside her. Not even the desire to protect her daughter could withstand the pure horror exploding from within. The little girl winced as her mother screamed, dread covering her like a blanket. The monsters would surely find them now.

The heavy blanket lifted, though, making her feel light as air. Her mother moved, scrambling out from underneath the wagon. She was still screaming, horrible shrieks pulled up from the depths of her soul as she fled. Was she abandoning hope, without her child? Or did she run because she had screamed, knowing that they had heard her, and running was the only way she could save her daughter now?

Either way, her mother didn't get very far before the Soulless seized her. Still miraculously safe under the wagon, the little girl's body shook with violent, fearful trembles, but she tried to focus on just keeping still and keeping quiet.

The minutes became hours, and the hours...there was no way of knowing just how long she was under there, but it proved a safe place. Slowly, the chaos started to dwindle, fading as fewer people remained. The little girl, weary and tired, allowed herself to cry, though she wept silently. The fires were calming down, not quite fading, casting the world in a light of burned amber before dawn. One night. Just one night had passed, and it took everything she had to hold back a whimper of indignant despair. If felt like days, but she was looking at only the first dawn of the rest of her life. Not even the birds were likely to sing this morning; all she heard were the quiet shuffles and placated groans of the Soulless milling around in the wake of their destruction.

Sweet, exhausted sleep swept over her, lulling her into a few hours of blissful ignorance. When she awoke, everything was bright and still. The whole ordeal felt like a nightmare, but when she rolled over onto her back to stare at the dark underside of the wagon, she was overwhelmed with reality. She began to sob, everything she held back gushing out of her, uncontrollable and wild.

The more she cried, the better she started to feel. Not only could she finally let so much go, but her continuing, uninterrupted sobs told her that she was safe. If there were any more of those monsters out there, they would have heard her. Sniffling, she rubbed her wrist against her eyes, smearing all the grime and salt across her cheeks, and she tried to push herself up. It took several attempts, her arms weak, as if her bones had melted. It was the same with her legs, though she eventually gained strength and crawled out from her hiding spot.

If she hadn't cried to the last drop already, the little girl would have wept for what had become of her home. The thriving, cozy village was now a barren wasteland. A few huts still stood like skeletons, but most were mere piles of rubble still smoking from the fires that brought them down. A sudden movement in the corner of her eye made her jump, but a quick, terrified glance revealed nothing more than a carrion bird, ruffling its dark, oily feathers before resuming its attempt to pluck a soft eyeball from a corpse's head. Her stomach lurched, and she threw up, a violent heave that spilled acrid vomit onto her shoes. Tears stung her eyes again.

Then she heard a groan, deep and throaty with a haunting dullness that made her stiffen with fear. Her hand stopped at her mouth. She knew she should turn around, but terror gripped her tight and held her in place. No, she thought desperately, they were supposed to be gone! Why now? Why not when she was crying? And what of the carrion bird? Why had they left it alone?

Crazily, she thought of just closing her eyes and letting the creatures take her. She had nothing to live for anymore. Everyone she knew was dead, her village was ruined. Her mother, her friends, the myth teller, they were all fodder for the Soulless now.

But she remembered all the horrible screams, imbued with more pain and fear than she'd ever want to experience.

And she remembered the words of the myth teller. She remembered the story of the hero, of the Savior that would only come in a time of great need. And she recalled her own words, in a voice so small and young, she could scarcely believe it had been hers not very long ago.

"I want to be the Savior of the Untouched."

"Then I will act the hero, and it will be so."

She drew in a deep, centering breath and let it out again in a whisper. "It will be so."

The girl turned, opening her eyes and forcing herself to look upon the destruction that had occurred. Just in time to hear another groan escape the walking corpse that lifted its arms, reaching for her. She pulled back, tripping over her own feet and falling to the ground. She stared at the impossible blue sky. It would be so easy to just stay there, but she fought hard against the temptation. She pushed herself up, scrambling back and away, narrowly avoiding the slow, clumsy reach of the Soulless.

With no time to think, the girl turned to run. Behind her, she could hear a second groan joining the first, along with the scraping effort of a broken body trying to get up. That was when she knew these weren't the Soulless that attacked the village. Everyone was changing; the dead bodies of the people she knew were coming alive again, but not as the people they were before. Those lives were gone forever.

And so was hers.

She didn't turn around that time. If she did, the sight of those familiar faces would render her incapable of doing what she must. Her friends, the myth teller, perhaps even her own mother. She repeated to herself a cadence to match her running steps: these people are all dead. These people are all dead. These people are all dead.

It wasn't easy to find her home among the destruction, but the girl recognized the bronze crest of her father's house among the rubble. Her heart surged as she danced over the ruins. The key to her salvation would lie here somewhere under the scorched wood and scattered rocks. She started digging, pushing everything aside, pieces of a childhood that seemed decades ago, threads of memory, shards of innocence, until she found the shine of a lacquered wood scabbard, cerulean blue, the color of her father's eyes. Her fingers were bleeding from the effort of moving the sharp stones and broken bits of wood, but she found it.

Wrenching the sword free, she was surprised by its weight and size. She'd never used it before, though she seen it expertly worked in the hands of her father. A wave of guilt hit her, knowing she would be using the weapon poorly out of desperation, but she pulled the blade from the scabbard. Nearly as large as she was, it gleamed impossibly pristine, and she tightened her grip on the hilt as she turned to face what was coming.

"Then I will act the hero," she growled, "and it will be so!"

The burdensome scabbard fell to her feet, and she charged forward to meet her fate. She could never forget that day, but she couldn't quite remember how she had the strength to fight them off the way she had, just a small thing with a sword too big, cleaving into the hungry Soulless as if she'd been fighting them her whole life. She didn't know what extraordinary power had helped her to survive. But that was the thing about heroes. They didn't become heroes by being ordinary.

CHAPTER ONE

The carriage rumbled through the mountain, shaking from all the ruts and rocks scattered across the rough road. Despite the jarring ride, though, the Slayer of the Soulless had been able to sleep, the rattling of the wheels becoming a strange lullaby that lured her into a much needed slumber. She could never sleep for long, though, opening her eyes to the golden landscape outside her window. The gentle peaks of the mountain had turned purple and blue in the sunset, a scene so serene it seemed unreal.

"Oh!" said a voice. "You're up."

The Slayer pulled her eyes away from the scenery, blinking at the darkness of the carriage. The young woman sitting across the way regarded her with a weak and worried smile. Her large, imploring eyes had been wide since the moment they met, down at the opening of the mountain pass, and the Slayer wondered if the woman would ever stop being so thrilled.

"Good," the woman continued. "I thought maybe you would sleep right through our arrival, but you've awakened just in time. We're nearly there."

The Slayer remained silent, not to be rude, but merely because she didn't know what to say. Conversation had never been a strong suit of hers, nor had she ever paid much attention to social graces. The young woman, clearly tormented by the silence as her face flushed red with concern, quickly added more, filling the space in with a stream of babbling. "I'm sure you're quite grateful for the rest, though. You likely don't get much of it, I imagine, but you'll find you have a very pleasant room awaiting you at the palace. A nice bed, a warm fire, a grand feast to fill your stomach." She turned her smile back on, charged with hope and anxiety, and a pride that seemed to waver slightly. "You will have comforts beyond anything else you've ever dreamed of, all compliments of the Baron and his wife."

Comforts like those simply did not exist in the Slayer's world. They existed in very few lives indeed. She looked at the young woman plaintively, trying to think of something to say, since she knew that if she spoke her mind frankly, she would offend her current company. "I'm sure," she said carefully, "that the Baron will not let himself be underrepresented. He has already done well in his choice of escort."

The young servant of the Baron tilted her head thoughtfully at the Slayer, trying to parse any additional meaning in the words. If she found any, she spoke nothing of them, instead leaning forward and pointing out the window. "Look," she said, "you can see it now, just around the corner. Paravelle."

As the Slayer peered through the glass, the promised splendor of the approaching city rose over the edge of the cliffs. A wheel struck a hole, jarring the carriage around, but it continued speeding down the treacherous path with incredible speed, as if it could not wait to be back in the safety of the fortress's mighty walls.

To consider all the grand stories told of the place, the Slayer almost expected Paravelle to glitter like stars on a perfect black night. She expected the waters surrounding the castle to be sparkling and crystalline, so pure one would hesitate to even look at it for fear of tainting it. But sight was little more than a dull change in the scenery, nothing grand or remarkable about it. The purple mountains were far more majestic, and the waters were murky and brown, as stagnant as the squat little stack of stones called a fortress. She would much rather find herself in the thick and wild forests, the great and sweeping plains, the lush valley and the dangerous mountains. She knew she was alone in that thought, as the rest of the world saw those places wrought with danger and death. She could protect herself, though; the people of Paravelle could not. They would die out in the wide world beyond their unimpressive walls, just as she knew her soul would suffer and wilt if she spent too much time within. Already, she could feel something inside of her dying, a dull ache of dread.

"Veroh," she said, addressing the young woman without taking her eyes from the stronghold. From one of its great tall spires, she thought she saw a flash of light winking at her, but it may have been little more than the setting sun glinting off a pane of glass. "How many people would you say reside in Paravelle?"

"Oh!" Veroh lept at the chance to showcase her knowledge, just as the Slayer suspected she would. Keep her talking, and perhaps the Slayer could manage to get a grip on her thoughts. "A great many, to be sure, but I couldn't even fathom a guess at the exact number. Hundreds, perhaps a thousand? There hasn't been as many people arriving as there used to be, which may be a good thing. Our resources can only stretch so far. However many people there are, though, every one of them will be excited to see you. They've been celebrating all day, in anticipation of your arrival. I believe I can even hear them now!"

How dull did Veroh think she was? Between the rattling carriage and the thundering hooves of the horses, all that could be heard was their rumbling little box on wheels. "What do they have to celebrate?" she asked. "Have any of them even seen enough Soulless in their cloistered lives to know what I protect them from?"

At first, Veroh appeared petulant over the criticism, but her face lit with a small spark of irritation. Good, the Slayer thought. So there is some fire behind those vacant eyes. The Baron's servant wasn't completely void of her own feelings and emotions, though she was incredibly talented at keeping them back.

Veroh straightened her back, tossing her dark hair behind her shoulders. "Many of them have," she said, voice tight and restrained. She tried a smile, but it was forced and lacking any mirth. "That is why they have come to Paravelle, for safety, to escape the terror of the outside world. The Baron's own wife is actually a refugee from the south, you know."

And his mistress probably was, too. "Tell me about the Baron's wife," the Slayer said. She settled back, attempting to give her escort her undivided attention, though she couldn't help glancing out the window every so often, as if expecting something to happen. "What is she like?"

"The Baroness?" Veroh seemed surprised at her interest, but she was eager to supply the information, nonetheless, especially since it veered away from their previous topic. "She is a strong woman, for one so young, much like yourself, if I may say so. An attempt to describe a person will always pale in comparison to the actuality of that person, so I feel as though I couldn't do her justice. You will meet her soon enough, and I trust you will like her. Most everyone does."

"Mmm." The Slayer's hum was an impassive, untelling response, followed by a brief silence. She noticed that Veroh barely squirmed, keeping those wide eyes on her expectantly. "And the Baron? Tell me what you can about him."

"What is there to say," Veroh said, blinking her eyes and giving a simpleton's smile, "that isn't known already? He is a hero to his people, a strong and trustworthy leader. He is very excited to meet you, as well. The tales of your work have made it to many wonderful fireside evenings. I'm glad to see that so many of the words appear to be true."

The Slayer sucked in her breath to force down the urge to take the insipid and watery-eyed Veroh and shake her, or at least to go back to topic that, while they made her uncomfortable because she didn't have a ready response, they seemed to inspire some sort of personality. That was the thing with these people. With the Soulless, you got exactly what you saw, while people like Veroh were filled with so many nuances and falsity that she sometimes felt they were better off being left to a dismal demise. She sighed deeply, refusing to mask her annoyance and hide her irritation.

"I assumed there's a captain of the guard?" she asked, wondering if she should just be quiet. For all the prepared responses, though, the Slayer was not about to go into a place without knowing what to expect. There were still kernels of useful information somewhere inside Veroh's praising descriptions.

"Of course!" Veroh smiled again. "He's also quite young, but he has done a wonderful job training our army. A towering pillar that holds up our fortress. Broad shouldered, strong in the arm, we are confident that he could fend off any Soulless that might discover our haven. Of course, none ever will, but we have that security, just in case."

"If he is so powerful," the Slayer stared at her guide, "then why does he stay here in Paravelle, as if some blushing virgin to battle? Such a force could be used to help eradicate this plight instead of just defending against it."

"That is what you're for," Veroh answered with some hardness in her voice. She settled a challenging look at the Slayer, suggesting that perhaps the questions had gone too far off course.

When the Slayer said nothing more, Veroh's eyes dancing toward the window. "Look," she said softly. "We are nearly there. Can you see the gates?"

She could. She would have to be blind to miss them. The carriage turned, descending into the valley, and the gates slowly opened as they headed down the narrow bridge across the moat. The doors were tall, groaning with the effort of movement, and she wondered if their excessive size had any purpose other than to impress. They could not be scaled by most Soulless, but she'd seen some with claws, with a completely unstoppable hunger that inspired them to get through anything if it meant a meal on the other side. The only thing that could truly stop them was a wel-aimed weapon, usually her own

.

Her father's sword. She closed her eyes a moment and thought of it there, at her side, and drew strength from its presence. At the same time, she felt suddenly exhausted, constantly bound to the sword's own unceasing thirst for blood. Inside the walls of Paravelle, she would find no rest or relaxation, hounded by the need to slay the beasts that lurked beyond.

"As soon as we hit the main courtyard," Veroh was saying, "you'll see the people waiting. They have been celebrating all day. You can even hear them, can't you?"

She could hear them, great, raucous cheers like a gathering storm. Though she knew they were sounds of merriment and excitement, they seemed eerily similar to the screams of torment she was used to, just a few octaves different. It made her wonder exactly what they were celebrating. Yes, there were refugees from the outside world in Paravelle, but there couldn't be many. Most of the citizens within these walls had probably never seen a Soulless attack, not a major one, so she'd be surprised if any of them had any idea what she was even protecting them from.

On the other hand, myth was a powerful force. Through legends, like the ones she remembered being told as a small child, people who had never seen a Soulless still knew them to be terrible creatures. Any description was vivid enough to inspire nightmares in any active mind, but they could never truly convey the horrific reality of the beasts. She envied them that ignorance.

"Are they really so excited?" she wondered, turning to Veroh now with dull intrigue. "Just to have me arrive?"

There was nothing contrived or insipid about Veroh's smile in response to that. It seemed radiant with an eager hope, genuine in a way that had yet to be seen from her. "Of course they are," she said, her voice a sigh of awe. "You're a living legend. I can't tell you how many of our own desire to do what you do, but can't imagine the sacrifice it must take. I shouldn't have to tell you; you'll see it for yourself."

As they passed through the gate, the Slayer closed her eyes again and settled back. Her ears had always been a little more trustworthy than her eyes. She listened for the sound of the rumbling wheels, and then shoved it back into the recesses of her mind, so that she could listen beyond it. It was the same method she used in rough weather, during attacks, whenever other sounds might mask the all-important signs of the Soulless in approach. Though the rain pounded, or the lightning flashed, or fires crackles and people screamed, she could listen past it, for the shuffling, the shallow breathing, the gentle moans. Finding the singing voices through carriage walls was no difficult task. It was raucous, boisterous, and primitive, but, under that, there was a sweet tenderness, probably from the mouths of children. She frowned, feeling strangely unsettled. She didn't deserve their cheers. Hero though she was, she was also a monster, a killer, a heartless scavenger, just like the creatures she saved them from.. They saw none of that desperation, that drive, that hunger, only the grand legend.

"Ignorance," she murmured, "is indeed a blissful thing."

"What was that?" Veroh asked, tilting her head a little and frowning as if missing a single word from the Slayer's mouth was the ultimate of failure in her job.

"Nothing," she said. She opened her eyes and peered through the window, careful not to lean forward too much. She could see the tops of heads and fluttering banners, but she could not see the people themselves, which meant they probably couldn't see her, either. For all they knew, the carriage was empty and they were cheering for a lie. And that was just it, wasn't it? The people of Paravelle had been told that the Legendary Hero was in that carriage, and they believed it to be true, because they had faith and hope and all the things that had died inside of her and anyone else out there in the harsh reality of the world.

"Don't worry," Veroh's voice broke through her reverie, and she realized she had her hands balled up into tight fists in her lap. "You won't have to see them now, unless you want to. I know the Baron was hoping to make your appearance a big event at the feast."

Feast. Even just hearing the word made her stomach twist, and her hand went to consciously cover her belly in turmoil. "Good," she said. "I don't think I'm in much of a condition to be receiving the masses right away."

"Of course not," Veroh agreed. "You will doubtless require a bath and some clean clothing first, and I imagine a small rest would not be out of line, either."

The Baron and his court. Feasts. Castles. These were things from a world completely unknown to the Slayer, and it made her shift uncomfortably where she sat. The carriage stopped abruptly, pitching her body forward, and things seemed to go incredibly quiet, even with the crowd still cheering outside. "We're at the gate to the royal courtyard," Veroh explained. "They're opening it now, and, once we're inside, we'll exit the carriage and meet with the Baron briefly."

The Slayer gave a stiff nod, listening to the sounds of the clanking portcullis. It struck her that the guards were moving forward, creating a barrier around the carriage and the gate, to keep the swarming masses away, and her stomach twisted tighter. They weren't ravenous for brains and body tissue, but the eager crush of the crowd reminded her far too much of the Soulless, clamoring to get through to her, piling up against each other. Those kept outside will always hunger and crave what is within.

As the carriage lurched forward again, a shiver wracked her spine. The lurching helped hide the reaction, and she could maintain her stoic, unperturbed expression. The creaking portcullis started to groan as it was lowered, accompanied by shouts from guards, and they crept forward slowly, sounds cushioned by the thick walls surrounding the courtyard.

Veroh smiled brightly as the carriage stopped. "We're here," she chirped, gathering her skirts. "Now, listen carefully. I'll exit first. The Baron and his court are waiting outside, and I will announce you. When you exit, you will be greeted first by the Baron. He will offer his hand, and you will kneel down and kiss his ring. The Baroness will do the same, and then the magistrate and the counsellor will kneel to you once you stand again. After that, your cadre will take you to your chambers. These girls are here to tend to you and take care of you. Whatever you need, they will strive to ensure that it is done. Are you ready?"

All the information swam in dizzy circles in her head, and she couldn't help noticing the foolishness of so much ceremony. Do this, do that, and to what effect? It was all pointless, meant to give off some signal of imaginary importance. It made her want to refuse such nonsense, but this was their world now. She had to play by their rules, convoluted and pointless as they seemed. Veroh opened the door, and the Slayer reluctantly stood.

What happened next was something of a blur for her. There was the Baron and his wife, and, behind them, a large entourage of scraping, reaching courtiers. The way their glossy eyes held a clear hunger for glory almost made her draw her sword, they were so much like a Soulless horde, but better dressed and with fewer parts falling off. She stopped herself, stayed by Veroh's voice lilting boldly over the crowd. The Baron, a man headed quickly down the slope toward old age with thinning hair and a rounded stomach, spoke, but she could not hear his words. She found herself mindlessly dropping to her knees, brushing her dry lips against the back of his proffered hand. The Baroness seemed hesitant to do the same with a wilting look of pain marring her hard but pretty face. She seemed to suffer through every moment of contact and was flushed with relief when it was over and she could draw her hand back protectively to her chest.

The Slayer rose and the crowd kneeled. She felt her knees weaken at the mindless perfection of the action. Soulless outside, Mindless within. Sometimes she wondered what it was she was even fighting for anymore.

CHAPTER TWO

While it was certainly strange to be pampered, the Slayer found it surprisingly refreshing to be bathed, then resting on a large, soft bed. The bathing itself had been awkward, a cadre of young women twittering and fawning over her in the process. They gushed over how strong her muscles were and how beautiful her face was once they had washed away the grime. The dust and blood and dirt was so thick that the washing took three large tubs, and the first was black as pitch when she stepped out. The girls rubbed her down with a sweet-smelling oil of lavender; the ointment made her skin tingle, a strange but not unpleasant sensation. They then wrapped her in a loose gown of smooth silk and told her to rest for the next few hours. There was a large, wide bed, big enough for ten of her, covered in thick, soft blankets. In a large marble fireplace, a fire crackled merrily, so different from the flames she'd witnessed ravaging so many villages. A table had been laid out with a bowl of ripe fruit and a tray of cold meats and cheeses, more food in one offering than she'd seen in the last month. She resolved to pace herself, but the next thing she knew, she had picked all the grapes clean of their stems and was licking sweet juice from her fingers. Then she had fallen into a deep sleep mere seconds after her head touched the soft down pillow.

It seemed she had barely slept at all, though, when a knock awoke her. The gentle rapping was quiet and delicate, but it snapped her eyes open as abruptly as if it had been a boom of thunder. She had trained herself to awaken to even the slightest provocation, and it took her a second to recall where she was. She remained still as the door to the chamber slowly opened, admitting a soft-footed Veroh and her small army of maidens.

"Are you awake?" she asked, stepping forward. In the corner of her eye, the Slayer saw Veroh standing there, nearly unrecognizable in an elaborate gown of green silk. Her hands, in a shimmering pair of gloves, were folded demurely in front of her, and the soft dark curls of her hair were swept up in a storm of pins and blossoms. "We only have so much time to make you presentable for the feast. The girls have specific instructions. I shall return in an hour to escort you to the banquet hall."

By the time the Slayer sat up, Veroh had left again, in a rustle of petticoats and skirts. The girls had her hands, babbling away as they pulled her to her feet. She thought they were the same ones from before, but it was difficult to tell. They all looked the same to her, doughy and distant, pristine and untested. Their movements were a blur, strange and unusual, dressing and fussing and plastering paint on her face and rosettes in her short-shorn hair. She would have resisted, but she was so overwhelmed, thinking that this was not too dissimilar from being surrounded by Soulless. Even the pins that they stuck into her scalp were like nips and scratches. Were these people so removed from pain that they allowed it in ridiculous grooming rituals? She couldn't decide which emotion was stronger, her disgust or her envy.

At least the dress chosen for her wasn't the nightmare atrocity of lace and silk that Veroh had been wearing. It was still silk, true, but fashioned in a more practical way. The long, widening skirt offered mobility, the waist cinched not too tight. The high bodice and long sleeves served well so that the breastplate of gleaming armor did not chafe. The conjunction of armor with a gown was ridiculous, but intriguing. A fine costume, she thought, as the girls fixed the ornate helm on her head, to suit their idea of a hero, though it hid all their earlier work with her hair. Still, absurd as it was, she felt somehow empowered by the costume, like a statue or a portrait, a hero of legend.

The Savior of the Untouched.

"Would you like to see yourself in the looking glass, my lady?" A timid handmaiden looked up at her eagerly. The Slayer looked back at her pale face, her wide eyes, her weak limbs. She wouldn't last longer than a minute out there with the Soulless, who would revel in digging their teeth into her soft flesh.

"My sword?" she asked. "Where is it?"

The nearest girl sent a skittering, nonplussed glance to her companions, who looked just as uncertain. "You won't need the sword for a banquet, my lady," she said timorously.

"Unless you plan on using it to cut your meat," remarked a much braver maiden in the cluster. A few laughs slipped from the cadre, though most of them were too nervous to even titter.

The Slayer ignored this, lifting her chin as she met the first woman with a steely gaze. "Tell me," she said, "would you attend a feast stark naked, without a stitch of clothing?"

Her words shook a few more laughs out of the girls, though they were less confident when they saw no mirth in her stone countenance. "No," the maiden stammered, flushing pink enough to match her gown. "Of course not."

"That is how I feel without my sword," the Slayer said. "Naked. And I refuse to go to this feast naked. Where is it?"

The sharp words inspired a scramble, and two of the handmaidens brought the weapon forward. It took them both to handle it, and, even then, they nearly dropped it. The Slayer found the blade and hilt still attached to her belt, and she yanked it quickly, roughly, from the girls' hands. As soon as the familiar weight hung at her hips again, a significant portion of her distress seemed to fade away. It worked as a heavy counterbalance to this strange situation.

"Let's go."

One girl rushed forward to alert Veroh of their arrival while the others fussed about her skirts. They created a cloud around her, like mosquitoes, making last minute picks and pokes. The girl who had earlier made the joke moved closer than the others, leaning into to whisper to the Slayer. "It was the Baroness who suggested we confiscate your sword," she said, low so the others wouldn't hear. "The Captain of the Guard tried to convince her it would be a bad idea, like taking a bone from a famished dog, but she would not relent."

The Slayer frowned at the girl. She tried puzzling out the purpose of the information, how it might fit into the boggling political games these people played in their idleness, but the girl's face was blank, if a little defiant, giving away nothing. "That was very wise of him," she noted, wondering what she might have done if they had insisted on following the Baroness's directive.

Even without the sword, it would have been a bloodbath.

"He is very wise for his age," the girl said. The Slayer briefly wondered if she was fond of this captain, but no. There was a flash of contempt in her eyes, no great love there. "You should have Veroh point him out to you at the feast."

"As if he'd need to be pointed out!" another handmaiden joined in with a laugh. The Slayer was startled to discover that their conversation, despite the whispering, had still been overheard. "Once you see him, he can't be mistaken for anyone else."

"And he's always at the Baron's right hand," another chirped in. "The Captain to his right, the Baroness to his left. I wonder where the guest of honor will sit. I can't even remember the last time we had one!"

This sent another ripple of excitement through the handmaidens, making the Slayer wince. Just when she thought she couldn't handle another moment of their babble, Veroh appeared and a respectable calm settled over the girls. She looked the Slayer over appraisingly, her lips pursing a little when her eyes fell on the sword. "Very well, then," she said. "Let us meet your gracious hosts."

She rapped a gentle tattoo on the large doors at the end of the hall and, with the clanking groan of some mechanism, they slowly opened. The music was the first thing she noticed--when was the last time she'd heard music like this, so soft and beautiful?--then the rumble of conversation and laughter. The bright colors were an instant assault on her senses, glowing light spilling through the opening doors from the grand chamber beyond. Blues and oranges and purples, all fluttering by like a storm of butterflies. The only color that seemed remotely familiar was red. She felt a sway of vertigo, but forced herself to stand strong. The last thing she needed was a show of weakness.

A man, large with a rotund stomach, called out over the crowd, his voice booming over the noise. "Announcing the Great Warrior, the Slayer of Soulless, the Savior of the Untouched!"

By the third title, an incredible hush had settled the chaos, all activity ceasing as heads turned toward the entrance. Veroh was doing a poor job of hiding her beaming pride as she nudged the Slayer forward. She moved, blinking owlishly at the crowd that stared back.

For a horrible moment, she did not see the well-dressed lords and ladies, but, instead, the hollow, hungry eyes of the Soulless. Grim and grey, never satisfied, those eyes haunted her and she saw them reflected in the empty faces of Paravelle. She nearly reached for her sword, half-expecting them to lift their bangled arms and shuffle toward her, mouths gaping open in anticipation of her flesh. But when they lifted their arms, it was to clap their hands, and, when they opened their mouths, it was to let out cheers and shouts.

She sucked in a deep breath to keep from being overwhelmed, her head swimming with confusing, conflicting images.

It took far more bravery and courage to step forward and face this lot than it did to confront a whole swarm of Soulless. An escort was immediately at her arm, gesturing for her to accompany him down the stairs. In perfect formation, like a flock of colorful birds across the sky, the handmaidens fell into place behind her and the crowds parted before her.

"Ah, so!" The Baron lifted his arms in greeting from where he stood behind a long table covered in colorful cloth. He looked even more polished than when she met with him earlier, his clothes richer in detail, his rust-colored hair styled with wax to match the turned corners of his small moustache. "Our guest of honor has arrived! Let us now feast!"

The cheer that rose up was deafening, as bodies began to move effortlessly, innately toward the proper places. Though she knew not what she was doing, the Slayer found that she, too, moved without thinking, trying to focus on the few things she knew in the sea of strangeness. Veroh took a seat on the far side of the Baroness, trussed up in so much finery that she seemed unreal. The Baron was jolly in his velvet doublet, which made his large belly seem even more obscene. And she discovered that the handmaidens were correct in being able to recognize the Captain of the Guard when she saw him, as she was being escorted to be seated at his side.

What struck her most was the pure, impossible beauty of him. Her world was one of constant ugliness, well beyond the horror of the bloodthirsty Soulless. The only beauty left existed in the awe-inspiring facets of nature and very few other places, until that moment. He was a slim, dark man, his shoulders decorated in the crisp cold decor of his neat military uniform. Under the glittering lights of a thousand candles, the thick black hair on his head seemed burnished with bronze, and he regarded her with the deepest eyes she had ever seen. Bright and full of life, they held her breathless, reminding her of a past she'd nearly forgotten existed. He was completely untouched by the harshness of the world. The shock was so great that she nearly had to be pushed down into her chair.

Though the guests were all seated, the flourish of activity continued. Servants began to fill cups and bring plates around, the musicians struck up a lively tune to match, and murmured conversations started to rise from the tables in a growing Buzz. The Captain of the Guard leaned over to whisper to the Slayer underneath the din.

"It is such an honor to meet you."

She stared at him, afraid to breathe, because when those intense smiled at her, all she could think of was how much the Soulless could desecrate there. "Thank you," she said, her shoulders drooping inward over a plate that revealed itself to be little more than greens and vegetables hidden under too much dressing and garnish. After just one bite, she knew she would have to dig beyond the too sweet sauce and dig out the more palatable radishes and carrots. Already, her stomach churned, and it was just the first course. She looked up at the sea of heads bent hungrily over the plates, food stuffed in, mouths open with laughter, brutal and garish.

She knew then it would be a long night. She tried to focus less on the food, especially when the hunks of roasted, bleeding meat were set out in front of her, and more on the strumming of the small band of mummers brought in to entertain. Music was one of the few things she found herself frequently missing, since the tune of the rain on the scorched earth grew tiresome after a while, pleasant though it was. Nature made beautiful music that called to her sense of a world without the madness of humanity, but the music played by other people often reached a part of her rarely touched. These were sounds only humans could make, in tugs and blows that struck only human chords. Everything else about the feast turned her stomach, but the music. Oh, the music…

Between the fourth and fifth course, there was an intermission for dancing, and she blinked up in dull surprise when the Captain of the Guard offered his hand. "I don't imagine you do much dancing in your travels," he said, with an odd twinkle in those startling bright eyes, "but I was wondering if you might do me the honor?"

She stared at the offered hand, the gentle open palm, the fingers slightly curled upwards. When she turned her head to glance around at the crowd, they had already risen from their seats to congregate in the open space in the middle of the chamber. The Baron and his wife led the way, his uproarious, boisterous laugh unlike anything she'd ever heard before. And there was Veroh looking at her, trying to speak with her raised eyebrows, though the Slayer couldn't tell if it was encouragement or warning. A few other heads turned their way. Her heart raced. Expectation? Or disappointment?

Why should she care? How could anyone stand these ridiculous human rituals?

Finally, she took his hand, allowing him to lead her onto the dance floor. She flinched when his other hand reached for her, until she realized he was creating the posture held by the others spinning around them in a flurry of curious looks and billowing skirts. He guided her hand to his side before settling his on her hip, and with the other hand, he held hers lifted to the side, stiff and unnatural, but mirroring the others.

"I'm sorry," she apologized immediately, though she bitterly resented feeling as though she should. "I've never--"

"It's okay," he said. "Just follow my lead."

He was taller than she expected, though she didn't have to look up much to gaze into his eyes and give a silent nod of agreement. There was a faint pressure against her side, and they started moving to the music, swept up in the flow of the others dancing around them. She thought she would be focused on trying not to mess up her steps, but she found herself instead intensely aware of the warmth of his hand. Even through the stiff silk of her bodice and the thin metal of her breastplate, she felt her skin tingle, her body flushed with a strange sensation that she hadn't known before, one she very firmly disliked.

The Captain of the Guard attempted conversation as they swirled and turned in a sort of haze. "Tomorrow, when you visit our barracks, I hope you will be pleased with what you find. The soldiers are very excited to have you stop in on a training session, give them a few pointers, perhaps."

Each sentence came out slight staccato, pauses she was expected to fill, but she didn't know how. "My," he said with a faint, bashful smile, "but you are a woman of few words, aren't you?"

Few words, indeed. After he realized that she was not in a conversational mood, he gave up, and she resigned to dancing, as well as she could. The music she had so enjoyed moments ago now seemed tedious and redundant, and when it finally did finish, she was handed a drink of water so satisfying that she longed for more than just the sip she was offered. She sought after the young maid who served the beverage, but was drawn back to her table for more of the feast.

At least the next course was light, though it was a shame that the entertainment wasn't the same. It was time, it seemed, for grandiose speeches. Grandiose and boring, most of them from puff-chested men or wan-looking women spouting empty accolades to the Baron and the Baroness and Paravelle. It then developed into irritatingly insincere soliloquys on how honored they were to have the great Slayer of the Soulless here among them, those who probably couldn't tell a Soulless from their grandmother until it was gnawing at their arm. More food arrived, more meat and something far too sticky-sweet, and she marveled that so much food could exist in just one evening.

Then came the Baron. He glowed in the cheers of the crowd for a moment before he lifted his beefy hands to quiet them. "Thank you, thank you," he said, "and let us thank our auspicious guest, too! Tonight, as we feast and celebrate her arrival, it is easy to forget why she is here in the first place. Is there so great a cause as this? Due to her strength and skill and fearlessness, Paravelle has been able to strive while the Soulless continue to ravish the world in their tireless hunt. Tomorrow, we must turn our eyes to the plague and the reason why we have brought her to us, but tonight we have been able to enjoy a life without fear or tyranny. My humblest grace and gratefulness go to the Savior of the Untouched, and to you all for creating this experience. I do hope she finds it to her satisfaction?"

There was the lifting lilt of a question in his voice, but she could only stare when they all looked her way, expecting an answer and likely another flowery speech. She knew she should say something, but a noncommittal could was all she could come up with at first. Clearing her throat, she tried again.

"Yes," she murmured, wishing she knew what to do with her hands. "Thank you. Your hospitality has been…"

She realized too late that she knew no word for it. She faltered, but, thankfully, the Baron forged ahead. "And tomorrow," he declared, "we will take the steps to lead Paravelle to its next stage of glory! Let us be dismissed so that we may be well rested to take on the next age ahead of us, like the shining beacon of hope that sits here at our table!"

With the emphasis that the Baron had given, she expected the response to be uproarious, but the applause was tired and bored and polite. People rose from their seats, milling about, some even heading to the exits. She was still too stunned by the proceedings to even move until there was a whisper in her ear.

It was Veroh, and the Slayer jumped a little in her skin, surprised that she hadn't noticed the young woman approach. Surprised and angry. If she hadn't been here in this strange delusion and Veroh had been Soulless, she'd be dead right now. She couldn't remember the last time her guard had been lowered so much, and she didn't like it at all.

"We can accompany you back to your chamber now, if you would like," she said, hesitating as thought trying to choose her words very carefully. "Many people choose to linger about and socialize, and I'm sure they would love to have a word with you. They will likely understand, too, if your journey has left you weary. The decision is yours to make."

She took one look around, and that was all she needed. One look at all the faces, laughing too loud, touching too much, all of them completely oblivious and defenseless against the terror outside their precious walls.

"Yes," she said. "It has been a long journey indeed. I believe I will retire. Thank you, Veroh."

Anything to put an end to this strange, odd nightmare. Veroh nodded, signalling for the swarm of handmaidens to come and accompany her back to her chamber.

⍰

CHAPTER THREE

Only once in her entire life had the Slayer slept so deeply, when she had been exhausted and frightened beneath an old wooden cart. Bright sunlight stabbed her like a sword when Veroh threw back the curtains from the window, piercing into her and jolting her awake. She reached for her weapon, never far away, ready to scramble to her feet and defend herself from whatever danger might be present, until her brain caught up with the reality of her situation. She was here in Paravelle, where there were no Soulless to fight, and she resided in that unfamiliar place known as safety. Her mind reeled, struggling to come to terms with the strange sense of vertigo and displacement.

"Bad dream?" Veroh asked. The young woman seemed fresh and new in the blur of the Slayer's perception, standing with her hands folded before her, a bright blossom of a flower springing up from a harsh landscape of jagged rock. She made for a much more pleasant awakening than the ones the Slayer was used to, though it was still jarring and strange.

"No dream," the Slayer murmured, hand to her dull head. She was glad for the lack of dreams, though, which served no purpose other than to interfere with the necessity of slumber. She pulled back the covers and slipped out of the bed, looking around for her armor, but she could not find it. Her eyes flashed to Veroh, a small burst of panic igniting in her gut.

But Veroh just smiled vaguely. "Your coterie will be here soon with a washtub and your clothing," she said. "We have a very busy day scheduled for you, and we're getting a late start. First, the Baroness would like you to join her for her afternoon tea, and then I'm to take you to the barracks, where you can meet with the Guard and offer your sage experience to improve them. They are exceptionally thrilled to have you visit."

Before they could say much else, the doors burst open and a steady stream of chaos poured into the room. As the handmaidens swept the Slayer up in a deluge of bathing and primping and dressing, Veroh stepped aside, keeping her eyes on a small pocket watch in the palm of her hand. She regarded it distastefully before slipping it away when the young women had finally finished. "We could stand for a little more hast and a lot less chatter, girls," she warned, then stopped to give the Slayer an appraising look. She gave a thoughtful hum and nodded. "Very well. Allow me to escort you to the Baroness's tea room."

The tea room was located high in the tall tower over the Slayer's room, where an elaborate system of private chambers for the Baron and his wife were built. It was large, but cozy, the stone walls draped in colourful tapestries, many of them torn or frayed or slightly faded, signs of a time long past. One wall of the curved tea room held tall, gleaming windows that looked out over the lush side of the mountains. Were windows like these what caught in the light as she arrived? As they entered the room, the Slayer saw the remarkable view first, then the room itself, which seemed strange and unnatural when one considered the glorious wilderness outside. Veroh excused herself, ducking away and leaving the Slayer alone with the Baroness, already seated on a long, low couch near the windows. She gestured to a similar chair across the way, a round table between them, where a mismatched tea set sat waiting.

"Thank you for joining me this afternoon," the Baroness said. "My husband sends his regrets for not being able to join us, but he has business to attend to. A cart of supplies just arrived from one of the foothill villages, and there's no rest for a man in such a position. Part of me is glad, though. This way, we can have a much more personal intercourse before you must focus on your own work with the Guard."

Even out of her ballroom finery, the young Baroness made a regal picture, poised and proper with an expression of grace and cleverness. Her eyes were bright and quick, following the Slayer as she moved across the room to the empty couch and perched awkwardly at its edge. The Slayer eyed the tea set, the finest she had ever seen, though hardly any of it matched. There was not a chip to be found on any of the delicate pieces, a rare thing indeed. The Baroness noticed the attention to those fine details and smiled proudly.

"Lovely, aren't they? Those matching white ones with the chrysanthemums are actually a gift from the Queen herself."

"Do you have much contact with the Queen?" the Slayer asked, not knowing what else to say. She watched carefully as the Baroness poured the dark tea into one of the chrysanthemum cups and passed it over. Feeling out of pace, the Slayer took it in both her hands, pulling it in close to breath in the pungent, earthy steam. Tentatively, she sipped at it, but it burned the tip of her tongue, spreading the unpleasant sensation through her entire mouth. She nearly dropped the cup, throwing it down as if it had bitten her, but she held back the urge, huddling around its warmth instead.

"No," the Baroness smiled lightly, "not much, but who does? She comes by every year or so, but her attentions are needed elsewhere. You know that much, I'm sure. She goes wherever the wind and necessity take her. We're not here to discuss the Queen, though. I am far more interested in you, Slayer of the Soulless. Your presence is a far rarer occasion than even the Queen's. I trust you enjoyed the festivities last night?"

The Slayer shifted, feeling restless with all this idle chatter. She could only think of time being wasted, for other things she might be doing. "It was different," she said, once she settled on a choice of words that would be truthful but inoffensive. "I am not accustomed to such pageantry. In fact, when a village feasts in celebration of victory over an attack, I am often back on the road or using the opportunity to rest and heal my wounds."

"I can't imagine it's an easy life out there," the Baroness said, her dark eyes resting on the Slayer strangely. It brought to mind the mountain cats that stalked the foothills, who would stare the Slayer down on the rare occasions when their paths crossed. It was a weighty, judging expression, attempting to determine the worth of one's prey. Usually, the cats were clever enough to leave her be, but she could rarely depend on humans to be so smart.

"Have you ever considered settling down?" the Baroness continued. "Surely, you've paid your dues. We would happily welcome you into our court, where you can impart your wisdom to the people and earn your well-earned retirement. Don't you ever feel the yearning to finally put up your sword and experience the peacefulness and quiet you fight so hard to protect for others?"

The Slayer lifted her eyes to the tall windows beside them. "Out there," she said, nodding to the mountains, "there is no such thing as peace and quiet, so I cannot rest. Maybe one day, it will be as safe as Paravelle, but, until that day, I must keep on."

"Aren't you in the least bit tempted?" The Baroness now wore a crooked, coy smile, her words thick as though filled with the persuasion the Slayer needed. "Just think on it, for a brief moment. To sleep as you did last night, inside four walls on a soft mattress, woken by the sun through your window rather than a Soulless at your throat. To never have to guess where your next meal will be coming from. This is the life the ancients lived, and it's right here, Slayer, right within your reach."

The Slayer allowed herself a moment to think on it, only to have her stomach clench in distress. "I couldn't," she murmured, her mouth suddenly dry. "Not until my job is done."

"Your job may never be done," the Baroness said, lifting an eyebrow. "Not in this lifetime, anyway."

"No," the Slayer admitted. "It won't. But I don't do this for myself. There are times, I will admit, when the temptation almost has me, but those are times when I am beaten, bloody, and broken. When I feel as though I can't move on, when it seems so much easier to just let them finally take me. When I can't move, when every inch of my body screams out in pain, or, even worse, when I can't feel anything at all. That's when you start to wonder if you're even alive, if that's how it feels when you start to make the transition from a living, breathing human being to a cold, starving Soulless. Have you ever felt that before, my lady? To be so numb as to think yourself undead?"

Silence stretched out between them as if for miles, interrupted only by the harsh call of a crow somewhere outside the windows. The Slayer felt a grim satisfaction in the Baroness's quiet response, pale and shaking with a hand to her throat. "No," she finally managed to choke out, breath finally released in a sigh. "I can't say I ever have."

"Veroh tells me you came from the south," the Slayer pressed on, "so you must understand the horror that's out there. There are many that can fight, many who cannot rest until every last Soulless is destroyed, and I am one of them. It is because we do not stop at the first glimpse of comfort, because we don't put up our feet and our swords the moment peace is suggest, that you and the Baron, Veroh and all those twittering little handmaidens she has flocking around me constantly can enjoy this peace. Until they are completely destroyed, I have to fight, so that more may enjoy what you have here. But that path is not for me."

"But there are others, aren't there?" the Baroness implored, gaining a bit of her color, though she remained breathless with awe. "We would have never gotten to this point if there weren't others to fight on and defend our world as well."

"Nor can you remain like this without us," the Slayer said, "and the more pillars to support a roof, the stronger it stands. Besides, this is the life I have chosen, the only one I've known. I wouldn't know what to do with peace and quiet. I would likely go mad."

The truth of the matter was that there was no question about it: insanity was all a place like this had for her. She could already feel it creeping under her skin, her fingers itching for a reason to reach for her sword. The Baroness was watching her with a thoughtful expression, head tilted, youthful eyes seeming to search for something, but what? Could this woman see the beads of sweat springing up on her forehead, despite the coolness of the room? Could she hear the steady thumping of the Slayer's heart, which seemed to grow louder and more persistent in her ears with each passing second? Could she ever imagine the vision that danced before her eyes in moments like this, when anyone she saw, she saw being torn apart and consumed by the Soulless in her head?

She must not have noticed a thing. The Baroness's contemplating look made way for a gentle smile. "Well," she said, "you can't claim we didn't ry. The offer will remain on the table, though, should you change your mind. You will always be welcome to our court."

The Slayer had nothing to say. It wasn't the first gesture of open arms she had received from well-intentioned leaders, nor the first she'd refused, but it was easily the first that left her feeling unsettled. The Baroness still watched her with those predator eyes, though her smile was soft and benign. What sort of welcome might she truly expect from this woman? It would likely be the same welcome a lioness might offer a young, springtime fawn.

Closing her eyes, the Slayer tried to banish that image from her mind, to dispel the gruesome carnage that made the blood rush to her head too quickly. It didn't do much good, though, as her eyelids were awash with violent red. "Thank you," she said, breathing out slowly to quell the powerful emotions surging through her, bubbling up from her gut. "I shall keep your kind off in mind. It may just come in handy someday."

"I'm not sure if I should hope for such an occasion or not," the Baroness said with a strange laugh that did little to take the edge from the Slayer's nerves. Thankfully, the door to the tea room slowly opened, the bell affixed to it jangling merrily to announce Veroh's cautious, docile entrance.

"Excuse me," she said, staying near the door and nodding to each of them reverently. Her hands were folded in front of her again, the perfect picture of attentiveness. "I'm sorry to interrupt, but the Captain of the Guard will begin training with the soldiers soon. I was wondering if the Slayer might be ready to join them to witness the operation."

Only after the Slayer had risen directly to her feet did she realize her eagerness to part ways with the Baroness might have been a little obvious. Her host drew in a sharp breath, her face souring a moment before it found its gentle, pleasant smile again. "So soon?" she asked. "My, how the time does fly!"

"I could come back later," Veroh suggested, her tentative gaze drifting between the two of them. "Perhaps that will give them time to warm up, so the Slayer will see them at their absolute best."

"Don't be foolish, girl." Turning up the brightness of her smile, the Baroness rose to her feet, a fluid, graceful motion that seemed to require no effort at all. That smile, on the other hand, seemed clearly strained, combatting the sharp glint in her eyes. "If she is to see our army and improve upon them, then she shall have to see them at their worst as well as their best. We were just finishing here, anyway, weren't we? We can perhaps continue our little chat during dinner tonight. It will be a much more intimate affair than last night's feast."

The Baroness looked to the Slayer expectantly, but, if she was to speak some word or give a kind gesture, she had no idea what it would be. She stiffly nodded to her host.

"Thank you," she ventured, then lost herself after that point of common courtesy.

An awkward pause followed, the Baroness's brows lifted as though she expected more, and all the Slayer could do was stare. Veroh coughed, a gentle clearing of her throat, ending the strange moment to divert their attention towards her. "Shall we go, then?" she asked, with an edge of impatience to her voice. "I imagine you won't want to miss a thing."

"No," the Slayer managed, starting forward. "I wouldn't."

Veroh was reaching for door handle, when the Baroness called out to them. "Wait," she said. "Just a moment."

But as the two women turned toward her, the Baroness appeared to have forgotten what she was going to say. Her mouth hung open, her finger poised in the air, ready to depart some great knowledge, but the words were frozen, somehow stuck, on the way out. Then she dropped her hand, closed her mouth, and shook her head. "Never mind," she said, sitting back down on her couch with a strange, placated smile on her face. Her hands rested in her lap, and her bright eyes seemed to glisten as she looked at them. "I'll not keep you. Have fun. I hope you find your visit with the Guard to be very...enlightening."

A horrible chill crept over the Slayer as Veroh ushered her out. It may have just been her imagination, but she could swear she could feel that cold, penetrating gaze digging into her even after the door was firmly closed behind them.

CHAPTER FOUR

In the coolness of the darkened halls, the Slayer began to realize just how odd the encounter with Baroness had been. "What a strange woman," she said as she followed Veroh through the twisting halls and down the spiral stairs. "Is she always like that?"

Though she did not stop moving, Veroh tilted her head as she might if the two of them were involved in a much more intimate, stationary conversation. "What do you mean?"

It was asked in a cautious way, as if Veroh already knew what the Slayer had meant, but did not—could not?—want to admit it. The Slayer glowered at Veroh's back for a moment, but eventually revealed her thoughts. "She smiles often, but it does not reach her eyes. She seems set on a prize and desperately uses persuasion and kindness to try and get it, though she knows it would be easier just to go out and claim it as her own more directly."

The Slayer would have liked to have seen Veroh's face just then, even though she knew she was probably expertly keeping her expression free from what she really thought. What she really though was probably not at all what she said. "The Baroness believes in ruling with a gentle hand, just like her husband. These walls may keep the Soulless out, but it does not keep the people in. Who would want to go out there, though, when they are safe and protected by kind rulers, while the outside world only promises strife and hardship and cruel tyranny?"

"You mentioned that you yourself was from the outside, like the Baroness," the Slayer said. "How long have you been here?"

"Oh, not very long actually." Veroh turned her head enough that the Slayer could see her faintly smile, a slight blush to her cheeks. "I've been very lucky since I arrived, to be taken in so quickly by the court. I was not so lucky before then, so I am incredibly grateful."

"What happened before then?"

Veroh filled the next moment with a heavy hesitation, drawing in a slight, uncertain breath. Deciding what to say, no doubt. Then she sighed a bit, wearily, shoulders sagging as if the tale, even untold, exhausted her. "I'm sure you know the story very well," she said. "Our village was in an endless cycle of attack, protect, rebuild. Just when you start to feel safe and comfortable again, they return, tearing you back down to desolation. After we lost my mother and one of my brothers, we decided to finally leave, and we weren't the only ones. Of the many that departed, though, only a few made it. I was one of the lucky ones."

"Lucky?" the Slayer asked. "Or just strong? That's all it truly takes to overcome them, the strength to fight and the strength to carry on. Luck can only last for a moment, but strength will keep us going."

Her words seemed to have struck a chord, as Veroh lapsed into a thoughtful silence again. Their path had since straightened out, though there were many turns around sharp corners that left the Slayer feeling confused about their location. The fortress was so large, she thought she'd soon lose track of up and down. They passed many people, some of them peasants bustling about some task, some of them nobles idly drifting to occupy themselves, all of them giving the Slayer and her escort a wide breadth. Finally, though, the flickering light of the torches lining the walls made way for a natural burst of sunlight from the large windows overlooking one of the many courtyards. An open archway lead to an arena of sorts, trampled grass and dirt fenced in by four strong walls, with a flurry of activity occurring within.

"Speaking of strength," Veroh said, "we have arrived."

The purpose of the arena-like courtyard became very clear in an instant, filled with strapping young folks in mismatched armor, playing together in a cacophony of clashing steel and grunts of effort. Several rings were set up where pairs of soldiers sparred against each other, others forming a loose circle around them to critique and cheer. Even more popular seemed the crowded field of test dummies where the guards moved swiftly through the obstacles to practice dismembering and decapitating. The Slayer found herself intrigued by their showy style, which she doubted would be helpful were those lifeless mannequins reaching for them and trying to get through their tender flesh. She also found it strange that, though there were punctured and well-used targets lining one wall of the enclosure, she saw no bows or anyone looking to improve their marksmanship. She stepped out into the light, peering over the tall fortress walls to appraise the orderly operation with equal parts fascination and criticism.

"So there she is," came a voice off to the side. "The famed Slayer of the Soulless, the Savior of the Untouched. It's about time you came around to visit us."

The voice came from an older man so craggy he seemed to be part of the stone wall until he hobbled forward, away from it. He may have been much taller back in his prime, but now his height was stunted by a crooked stoop to his shoulders and an awkward limp, caused by the strange, make-shift leg on his right side. He peered at the Slayer with his thick brows bristling in thought, his left eye hidden behind a leather patch that did a poor job of covering a long, pink scar down his face.

Veroh jumped slightly, startled by the old man's presence, a hand to her chest. "Thom! I didn't see you there. Yes, though, this is the Slayer of the Soulless, don't you remember from the feast last night? Where is the Captain of the Guard? I would have expected him to meet us here when we arrived."

The Slayer didn't mind the delay, enjoying the chance to examine everything on her own accord first. She looked at the old man carefully, taking in all the markings of a warrior in his scars and his broken nose. "It's good to meet you, old man. Do you also serve on the Guard?"

Adjusting his weight on his cane, Thom snorted. "In my own way, I suppose," he grumbled, though there was a joviality to his voice. "Consider me more of a consultant, than anything, especially as of late. This current Captain actually listens to others on ideas and what have you, for someone so young. Paravelle has needed a captain like him for a long time now."

"What happened to the last Captain?" the Slayer asked. "And when?" As she spoke, her eyes roamed the arena for the young man who had danced with her the night before, but found him nowhere among the dedicatedly focused soldiers trying to show off for her eyes. One young man had paused long enough to grin at them...no, not at them, but just Veroh, who caught the glance and smiled faintly back, nodding her head. A lover, perhaps? Or, no. The soldier lifted his hand in a jaunty, playful wave, and the Slayer pegged him as a brother for the doting way Veroh's smile blossomed before she pulled it back to a serious line.

"Little less than two years ago, it was," Thom said. "Damn bloody fool. We were celebrating the Baron's sister's engagement to that Duke who rules the City on the Lake, and they'd sent over nearly half a dozen caskets of their moonshine swill as a gift. Potent stuff, that is, would take the paint right off the wall if you let it. So, this idiot, he gets blazing drunk, and falls to his death off the balcony off some tart's room in the east tower!" He shook his head as a bemused chuckle seemed to rattle in his chest. "Bloody mess, that was, in more ways than one."

"Thom!" Veroh hissed through clenched teeth. A faint red had covered her face, though the Slayer couldn't quite tell if it was embarrassment or anger that colored her in such a way. "You shouldn't speak ill of the dead!"

"Why not?" the old man scoffed. "What would happen, he'll rise up from the dead to feast upon my brains?" His hand reached out to find Veroh's, giving it a little pat. "Those days are long gone behind us now, girl, thank the stars."

Veroh pursed her lips, her cheeks burning red from either embarrassment or anger, it was difficult to tell, but she deflated slightly and found her way to a faint, watery smile. "I suppose you're right in that respect," she allowed, "but it's still rude."

"This one," Thom sighed dramatically, shaking his head sadly at Veroh before his eye swivelled toward the Slayer. "I remember when she first got here. They tried to get her into the Guard, but she was destined for something else entirely. Something even better, perhaps. This is the start of a new world where quick wit and gentle graces get you much further than swift moves and a mighty sword. Every day I see her, I can't help thinking of how proud her papa would have been."

"My father," Veroh explained, when the Slayer met her with a curious look, "made it to Paravelle with us, but just barely." She had to stop for a moment, choking something down, blinking a sheen of moisture out of her eyes. "It was almost as if he was holding on to life just long enough to see us safe. He took to a bed soon after we arrived and made it no further than the next moon. At least he made it, though. He was given a lovely funeral and a proper burial, in a fashion that we would have been unlikely to manage ourselves."

"Decapitation?" the Slayer asked, feeling a strange prickle on the back of her neck. "Incineration?"

The thought of the destruction that had inevitably befallen her beloved father's corpse made the color drain from Veroh's face. "Incineration, of course," she said softly. "This conversation has taken a rather unpleasant turn, hasn't it? I wonder what's keeping the Captain so long."

As if on cue, summoned by her question, the Captain of the Guard appeared, emerging from the door on the far side of the arena. A cloud had passed over the sun at that moment, but the world didn't seem to darken at all. It was kept illuminated by the sheer brightness of his smile, it seemed. His hair was tossled as if by wind, his helm tucked beneath his arm and resting against his hip. Even with the clean-pressed dress uniform replaced with the battered, mismatched armor that outfitted the Paravelle Guard, he still radiated with youth and innocence, with exuberance and energy. With him was another young man, with whom he exchanged a few comments before they reached the Slayer. He bobbed his head in a sort of bow, greeting her with a wide grin.

"It's finally time to get down to business!" he said, with the excitement of a child. "I haven't kept you waiting too long, have I? I just wanted to make sure everything was prepared. What do you think so far, Slayer of the Soulless? "

"Prepared?" The Slayer lifted an eyebrow. "A soldier should always be prepared, even at the moment when his guard is down. What would you have to prepare for, that you shouldn't have already had on the ready?"

The smile dropped so quickly from the Captain's face that she practically heard it shatter. He blanched, jaw hanging as his head tried to fathom a response. His mouth closed eventually, though, as he steeled himself in resolve against the rebuke. "You're right," he said. "Of course. But once you see what we have in store for you, you'll understand why I wanted to ensure everything was perfect. We're not used to such guests as yourself. That's no excuse, but we'd much rather you see us at our best rather than our worst."

"You don't need to impress me," the Slayer said, looking at him evenly to help her words hit her mark more clearly. "You only need to be strong and be willing to learn. I'd rather see you at your worst and know the problems you have than see you at your best and miss the chance to correct what is wrong."

"Once again," the Captain said, having regained his smile, his energy channeled into the balls of his feet; he seemed incapable of standing still, "the Slayer proves herself to be incredibly perceptive. Come, let us put that sword of yours to use! Surely, you have been wanting to use it. Train with my soldiers and give them your combat advice. We're all eager to learn everything we can."

She had to admit, her hand nearly ached to feel the hilt of her sword again, and she craved the familiarity of combat after the unnatural torment that had been afternoon tea. She nodded, allowing the Captain to lead her into the thick of the training yards, to better observe them and figure out how best to improve them.

Working with the soldiers proved a worthy endeavor. Untested as some of them were, they had a good grasp of the basics, the essentials, and some of them had survived Soulless before they found their sanctuary in Paravelle. They were exceptional, and they were few, most of them like Thom and unable to fight much anymore. Still, they were strong and eager, though she was often derailed from her demonstrations as they filled her ears with requests for stories and more questions than she could ever hope to answer. Quite a few times, she had to break away and exhibit the annihilation of one of the practice dummies to release her anxiety. All their eagerness and hunger made her feel as though she was back out there among the monsters, struggling to keep her head up.

"I can see why you've gained the prestige you have," Thom commented, when it was decided that a break was needed for everyone, to breathe and rehydrate. "I recall hearing about you when you first started carving your way through Soulless a long time ago. Even got the chance to see you in action, once. You remember a small village out west, near the Targatal Marshes, where we made our trade in peat moss fertilizer? Ah, you probably don't. All those settlements probably start to look the same after a while; I know they did when we made our way here. Point is, I saw you there and could hardly believe all that piss and vinegar came from someone younger than my own daughter, and look at you now. Bet you're even fiercer now than you were then, too."

The Slayer stared blankly at the old man, trying to wrap her head around the anecdote and a way to respond. Her eyes travelled down to the place where his false leg was, bolstered with pistons and gears to allow better movement, a fascinating display of mechanics. "Is that when you lost your limb?" she asked.

"What, this old thing?" he said, giving the mechanism a well-practiced flex. "No, no, much more recently than that. On my way to Paravelle, as a matter of fact. Good thing we were close, before the rot started to set in. Got myself finally bit by one of those bastards, you see, got right on into my calf and nearly tore the whole thing right off my bones. My daughter had to chop it off at my knee before the disease started to spread. Travelled the rest of the way here in the back of a wagon trying not to howl from all the pain, despite our companion's hand at medicine. Still hurts like a devil, truth be told, but this here metal leg makes it better. Brought in by the Queen's Engineer one time. Amazing what that woman can pull off in that great big ship of hers."

"I have to agree with you on that one," the Slayer said. "From what I've seen, she will only continue to make great things. I hear they're developing some interesting weaponry up there, too. If any of it turns out to be nearly as effective as mechanized limb replacements, we're in for some exciting times. Pity the Engineer doesn't have the skill of her great-grandfather, though, to make more airships. I'll never even guess how that hulking thing stays afloat as it does, and for so long, ceaselessly."

Something piqued Thom's interest, but, before he could express as much, the Captain had moved up to join them and interrupt. "You're not putting the Slayer to sleep with all your stories, are you, Old Thom?" he asked, though his tone was light and teasing and playful. "The way he tells it, this man is about as old as the very earth itself, but don't let him fool you. We have probably a good hour or so before we'll be expected to get ready for the evening repast, Slayer; would you like to engage us in a few more skirmishes and drills?"

The Slayer nodded. "Perhaps you can tell me more of your travels tomorrow, Thom," she said, "or of your life here in Paravelle. After all, I think I should like to know the story of that missing eye as well as your missing leg. Until then."

Tipping an invisible hat, Thom settled back against the cool wall of the barracks enclosure to get comfortable to watch the proceedings. "Until then," he agreed, and the Slayer went to get lost again in the swirl of excited swords and well-placed hits, thinking that if the Baroness had wanted to convince her to stay, this was how she should have done it.

CHAPTER FIVE

Later that evening, back in the comfort and quiet of her room with a stomach too stuffed with food, the Slayer found sleep quickly, almost as soon as her head touched her pillow. Such easy slumber did not happen often, and it kept her under for a good portion of the night. After a while, though, she began to stir, restless and troubled, old habits dying hard. A fire still crackling in the fireplace, casting weak, indistinguishable shadows around the room as she finally abandoned sleep and opened her eyes. She stared ahead, pondering this worrisome disturbance, wondering if there was more to it than her body's nature, unaccustomed to such peace.

Above her, floorboards creaked from someone walking, and she swore she heard breathing, but it could very well have been from her own lungs. She laid still for a long time, trying to reconnect with sleep, but to no avail, only growing more restless by the minute. Perhaps she needed a drink of water. Perhaps she needed to take a late-night stroll, especially since she was unaccustomed to resting so long. Her body wasn't used to this relaxation. She sat up, reaching for her sword as she climbed out of the bed.

The shadows shifted and, suddenly, something had her by the wrist, something cold and clammy and tight. She didn't scream, though her heart leapt into her throat. Without sparing a single thought for who it might be, she acted swiftly, swinging her fist, which met with the familiar feeling of the soft, decaying flesh.

Soulless.

There was a Soulless in her bedroom.

It staggered back from her punch, but it did not let go, dragging her down with an angry growl. She knew, with the way it continued to grapple with her and hold its own, that this was not some just-turned monster, either. She tried pushing herself up, but its body pressed down on her, clawing at her hair as if to get to her scalp better. She shoved the heel of her hand into its chin to hold it back as she groped for her sword in the darkness. There would surely be another coming; there were always more, and if she didn't control this one before then, she would be lost.

She hardly had the time to think. She had its wrist, but it still had her hair. It scrambled and scratched as if its brittle nails alone could slice through her skin, and it would try without ceasing until it succeeded. Finally, tough, she found her sword, found that familiar, well-worn hilt.

Difficult as it was to get the right angle, the Slayer drove the blade up through the Soulless' concave chest. It released a startled, gruesome sound that soon turned into a shriek of annoyance. The stab to the chest had only angered it, filled it with rage and increased its desire for her soft, warm flesh.

There was only one way to kill a Soulless, and she couldn't do it from here. She yanked the sword out of its chest and brought the hilt smashing into its face. Screaming in indignation, it staggered back, hands lifted to protect its precious head, but it would need more than hands to save it. She took the opportunity to scramble to her feet, the Soulless staggering up with her and fixing her with its dead gaze before it lunged for her again. She swung her fist again, connecting another punch, and then braced herself. It sometimes took a lot to smash through the skull, especially if one's aim was off, and this Soulless had not deteriorated much.

Her aim was true, though she wasn't aiming for the skull. She cleaved straight through the lifted wrists and the skinny neck of the pitiful creature with barely any effort. Two hands and the head fell to the floor with ragged thumps; the body would be a little further behind, a delayed response before gravity took over. The body hit the floor and continued to writhe, just as the fingers still tried to grasp her ankles, and the mouth still opened and moaned, as it would until she split the decapitated head at her feet into two halves, as easily as if she were cutting a melon. A rotten melon, to be sure, a putrid smell filling the room as the diseased brains spilled out onto the carpet. She struggled to breathe, suffocated by the overwhelming scent made worse by being indoors in close quarters, rather than out in the open air with the breeze to carry the noxious stench away.

The Slayer carefully controlled her breathing as she cleaned her blade with the nearest cloth, which happened to be the bedspread, smearing it with the strange black ichor that was the Soulless' blood. She did it quickly, knowing she had to find where the others might be. There was never just one; it was absurd to think there would be. And yet when she looked around the room, she was confronted only by still shadows and an unnerving quiet.

Frowning down at the decapitated body, she was struck with the strange reality of the situation. Not only was there a Soulless in her bedroom in one of the safest havens the world over, but there was only one of them, or so it seemed. Something was certainly not right here, and something awful crept up her spine.

The Slayer dressed quickly, keeping an eye on the body, despite knowing that she'd completely destroyed it. With each article of clothing and piece of armor she donned, her mind swerved and her stomach twisted with growing dread. Something was wrong, it practically screamed in her ear, echoing in her head as she noticed the stark, utter stillness around her. Something was terribly wrong.

When she threw open the door and charged out into the hallway, the whole castle seemed completely abandoned. No guards, no anything, until she heard the clatter of metal and a soft groaning somewhere along the way. Something hit a wall and slumped wetly to the floor, and there was a slight pause before the subtle sound of masticating and slurping filled her ear.

So there were the guards, though it was too late for them to help her now. Or for her to help them. She headed down the bend of the hallway where she heard the telling sounds and found the Soulless she expected to be there. They were easy to dispatch, distracted as they were with their feeding, digging into the stomachs of the guards. Her sword seemed to glow in the soft torchlight as she swung, slicing into the neck of the nearest one. Its head, grotesque and discolored yet still chillingly human, rolled toward her feet, and she stepped on it, crushing it under her heavy boot as the second one turned its head. Glassy eyes, about to pop from their sockets, stared at her blankly, hazy from the pleasure of feeding. It didn't take long to recognize the warm body in front of it, though, the vessel of meat even fresher than the one in its hands, and something sparked there, a flash of anger and hate and hunger. It hissed through its pointed teeth and lunged forward, hands ready to grip her and tear her apart.

When the creature rushed forward, it met the tip of the Slayer's sword, and kept moving, impaling itself in the effort to reach her. Quickly, she yanked the blade out, turning the grip in her hand so she could send another bloody head to the floor. She stomped down on the skull again, finding a strange satisfaction in the squishing sound of the brains splattering underneath her foot.

Again, the Slayer breathed out slowly, trying to collect her thoughts, before setting aside her sword for a moment to pull out her long dagger. She knelt beside the body of the first guard, trying to ignore the mess of intestines gathering in his lap. Already, the face that peered out from underneath his helm was mottled and yellow, the strange venom in the Soulless' bite leeching into his skin, but she could still see the innocence there, the shock trapped forever in his wide, dead eyes. She sighed, then shoved the dagger through his eyes, into his brain, jerking it around a little to make sure. She shifted and did the same to the second guard, ensuring that the two of them didn't come back again as the same Soulless that had killed them.

The Baron, she thought, as she hastily cleaned her weapons and tucked the smaller one away. I need to find the Baron and warn him of this. If it isn't too late.

Strangely, she encountered nothing else as she raced through the halls, trying to get her bearings and figure out where to go. The castle seemed to be under some heavy spell of sleep, its citizens slumbering away while a nightmare seeped in through the shadows. It seemed that perhaps those three were the only creatures, but that was impossible. Soulless always moved in large numbers, and where would those three have come from, anyway? She thought she heard some shuffling behind closed doors, gentle moans and sloppy feasting, but she couldn't stop. Whatever was in those rooms was gone by now; her main goal was to find the Baron.

As she neared the Baron's wing, a grisly and disturbing scene unfolded, the castle no longer so strangely empty and quiet. She passed a few more guards with their armor ripped away to reveal their tender bellies, a serving girl as well, blood smeared on the walls and her body pulverized into mush, but there was no sign of the Soulless the carnage. And no sign of anyone who could tell her where to find the Baron. She clenched her teeth together, clinging to her sword tighter. She swiftly ensured that the guards and the girl were properly taken care of, carving her way into their skulls, and then she prepared herself for a bold move.

"Hello!" she called out, wincing at the loudness and the desperation in her voice as it echoed along the hallway. A sound like that was guaranteed to call attention to herself, but she had to try, she had to know if it wasn't too late to save anyone else from this sudden scourge. "Can anyone hear me?"

A low groan responded from behind the nearest door, followed by the slapping of palms on the other side. Scowling, she prepared herself to wrench open the door and destroy whatever was on the other side, but a sharp, piercing scream cut through the air, high and muffled and very human. The door was an effective barrier for now, so she turned around to pursue the scream, maybe she could still actually save someone.

Thankfully, there weren't many doors in this area of the stronghold, or else she'd be playing a guessing game all evening. She was positive that the scream came from behind the large, ornate double doors behind her. The Throne Room.

She reached for the long, twisted door handle, stopping herself before throwing it open. She shouldn't announce herself too brashly; a bold entrance might distract the Soulless from whoever was screaming, but she had no way of knowing how many were inside, and she could be waltzing right into an ambush. She cracked the door open slightly, just enough for her and her sword to slip in.

She had barely two seconds to observe the scene before the door slammed shut behind her, not enough time to make any sense of it. Dozens of Soulless were scattered around the large hall, several of them deep in the process of tearing through the howling citizens. Many people had gathered helpless on the dais, frightened men and women, Veroh among them, adrift in the sea of carnage. It was strange that Soulless weren't attacking them all, but even more peculiar was the Baroness, standing at the edge of the dais with her arms spread out as if to guard her citizens. She was calling out to them, telling them not to worry, that she'll protect them, as Soulless milled all around her. Not a single one of them touched her, though, as if she was entirely invisible to her and the whole crowd of potential victims behind her.

When the Baroness saw the Slayer standing there by the doors, though, things became even stranger. Her eyes widened with a sudden flash of panic, and her consoling words stopped dead in her mouth. "You!" she gasped. "But how did you survive?"

One thing was clear: the Baroness had not intended to show her surprise. Her face hardened, her shock replaced with anger, and, perhaps so swiftly that no one noticed, she reached out to nudge the shoulder of a Soulless. The creature stopped, shifting its attention to where the Baroness now pointed, straight at the Slayer, and it let out a low groan of comprehension.

Before the Slayer could even begin to understand what had just happened, the swarm had shifted, dropping the bodies they currently consumed, and moving like a wave toward her instead, their new direction lead by the Soulless directed by the Baroness. The mindless, milling masses were being told what to do, and they were listening. They suddenly followed a vague plan, these creatures that only knew hunger and hate. And as they lurched forward under the Baroness's directive to attack, the woman still fielded her citizens behind her, chanting, "Don't worry, stay back, I'll protect you. I'll protect you."

CHAPTER SIX

What followed next was utter chaos, but chaos she could handle. The Slayer's whole life had been nothing but chaos, and she switched into her fighting form quickly, keeping her back to the wall so they couldn't completely surround her. It didn't help that her brain was reeling, turning somersaults to make sense of what she had seen on the dais, but her sword was soon slick with blood and gore. Bodies were falling around her feet, one after another swiftly and deftly put to death. The Baroness continued to plead faith out of the subject who cowered behind her, all the while giving subtle nods and gestures to send more of the Soulless toward the Slayer.

Sending them. They were taking orders from her, indirect as they may have been. Soulless didn't take commands from anything except their own base, primal instincts. Yet there they were, attacking to the demands of the Baroness like an army of undead, while she pretended to be protecting those who clearly she had not directed them to attack yet.

The Slayer had no time to think about it, though, only to fight back, hacking and slashing and ignoring the pain. A shout rose up from the Baroness, screaming lifting up as someone on the dais was grabbed by an errant Soulless and torn down to the floor, where a small swarm descended on the hopeless victim. "No! No, quick, everyone move away! Move away!" There was hardly anywhere to move, though, and, even from the other side of the room, the Slayer saw a spark of panic in the Baroness's eyes.

With her back to the wall, the Slayer wondered where all these Soulless could have come from, why the Baroness seemed to control them, and exactly what was going on around her. She was starting to feel overwhelmed when the large doors were thrown open, one of them clattering against the wall, the other finding a few Soulless in the way instead. The Captain of the Guard burst in, followed by a small retinue of his soldiers. "Baroness!" he called out, his eyes wild as he gripped his sword, panicked but ready. "The castle, it's--"

The words left him quickly. For a moment, he was held in place, shocked by the swarm filling the room, and half the Soulless shifted their attention towards the new distraction. Some of them abandoned their attack on the Slayer to pursue the Captain's army, and the Captain's army pushed through their surprise to start attacking back. As he hacked into the nearest Soulless reaching for him, he shouted orders to his soldiers. Some responded with alacrity and determination, though many of them were bungled and overcome by the situation. Their lack of experience was showing as vividly as a wide-open wound. Confronted with the nightmare of their childhoods, they forgot all their strength, and the Soulless overtook them easily. The Captain held his own, though his distress and confusion was palpable. "My lady!" he shouted over the din of the battle. "What has happened here?"

Despite the inexperience of some of the soldiers, the tides were turning, the number of active Soulless diminishing as they cleaved their way through. The palpable relief could be felt from the small crowd on the dais, though that was soon to change. At the center of it all was a small kernel of distress, radiating from the Baroness as she looked at the slayed Soulless is dismay. Her head slowly shook from side to side, but there were gears turning in her brain as her eyes danced about.

If the Slayer had chosen to look up at any other moment, she may have missed it. Fate, it appeared, was on her side. "You worthless imbeciles!" the Baroness spat, and her entire mood shifted. "Take them all, for all I care!" She shoved the closest person off the dais, into the few Soulless who still milled around them. A scream of shock rose up from someone else as their attentions shifted yet again, to the bounty that had previously been denied them. Hopping down from the dais herself, the Baroness took a hold of two Soulless by their shoulders, and started moving toward the back of the room, toward a small door set into the wall. "Kill them!" she shouted. "Kill them all! You two, you're coming with me. Destroy anything that gets in my way!"

"Captain!" the Slayer shouted over the new chaos; the innocent people the Baroness had been herding fell victim to the Soulless easily now, as none of the soldiers could reach them, and she realized that she had no direct line to the door. The Captain, however, was mu h closer. "The Baroness! She's escaping!"

Confusion flickered across his face, making him nearly susceptible to an attack, but he stabbed the Soulless swiftly. "Escaping?" he remarked, and she could tell that he was still blind to what was going on. He had missed the turn in her disposition, and anyone else who caught it was quickly being torn apart. Gritting her teeth, she tried to push forward, kicking away the Soulless on one side before throwing her elbows out to plow through them.

Not everyone on the dais was hopeless, though. Veroh shoved and pushed and kicked, letting out a small scream of surprise when a Soulless grabbed the skirt of her nightdress, but she tore away, leaving it with only tattered scraps. "I've got it!" she called out over the carnage. "I'll go after her."

"Veroh!" the Slayer shouted. She was undeniably the closest to the door, and she made it there quickly, but she was unarmed and knew not what she was forging into. "Wait!"

Still, there was no stopping the young woman, who wrenched open the door and rushed after her fleeing mistress.

"What's going on?" the Captain demanded.

"I'm about to find out!" the Slayer called back, letting her irritation flow into a firm kick that knocked a Soulless back into the other   s. How had they killed so many, and yet more seemed to seep out from the very shadows of the room? Finally, she reached the door, wrenching it open and charging into the darkness after Veroh and the Baroness, hoping that she wouldn't be too late. As the door closed behind her, the moaning music of the battle behind her seemed oddly muffled and distant, as though it was happening a million miles away. She felt like she had been dropped into a different world entirely, and she listened carefully for signs of where the others had run. She could hear Veroh's swift footsteps and panting breath, she could hear the moaning of the Soulless guards, and murmured curses by the Baroness, too far away to discern beyond her livid, panicked tone.

"Your Highness!" Veroh's shouts echoed down the long, dim passageway. "Stop, please! What's going on?"

"Veroh!" Wherever they were, at least Veroh had gotten the Baroness to stop, pleading with her. "Not a step closer or else you'll be feeding these disgusting monsters like all the others back there. Or it's not too late. You're a smart girl, that's why I've chosen you to help me with so much. You can't even begin to understand what is going on right now, but you might. You could benefit from all this, Veroh, just as you benefitted from your position in my court. Help me out of here, and I'll show you what I mean."

"Did you do this?" Veroh asked. "You kept the Soulless from attacking us. How did you...why?"

Just then, the Slayer rounded the corner, weapon ready for anything she might find as she happened across the Baroness. "Veroh, behind me!" she shouted, charging forward, ready to push the young woman out of the way if she had to, just as the Baroness, caught by surprise, ordered her Soulless guards to attack. They didn't stand a chance, though, cleaved in half, skulls stabbed, as she made quick work of disposing of them so she could turn her attention to the Baroness.

"What have you done?" the Slayer growled, crouched and ready to attack, or to rush after the Baroness if she attempted to flee again. She held the woman in a firm glare to paralyze her in the spot, her eyes dancing about for some sort of refuge or help.

"N-Nothing!" the Baroness stammered. She shook her head fiercely, as if trying to dislodge the memory of terror. "I swear it, I've done nothing! They must...they must have...Veroh, please! Tell her how I was trying to safe you, how they crept in through the night. The Soulless—"

"--have not penetrated Paravelle in over a hundred years." The Slayer tightened the grip on her sword. "Explain yourself. I saw you back there. They only attacked when you told them to attack. What is going on?"

"I-I don't know what you're talking about," she wailed, dropping to her knees and inching forward, reaching for the Slayer. "Please! You must understand—Veroh! Tell her!"

Veroh's voice came quiet and confused. "Is this true? Just now, if the Slayer hadn't shown up, those Soulless..."

"No, please!" the Baroness begged. "You don't understand!"

"I understand far more than you realize," the Slayer said and the Baroness, seeing the fury in her eyes, started to scream for mercy, belting out nearly unintelligible pleas. Her hands started to clutch at the Slayer's leg, but the Slayer, nudging into Veroh behind her, backed away. The wild begging halted quickly, as the Slayer brought her sword down through Baroness's neck, severing it and any hope for her salvation in one sharp move.   Her head hit the floor with a dull thump, and a silence hung in still air for a moment before the passageway echoed with the crunching of bone and the splatter of the Baroness's brains.

CHAPTER SEVEN

"You...you killed her."

The Slayer didn't have time for Veroh's shocked observations at the moment, kneeling down beside the body to search it for anything that might be helpful. The Baroness didn't have much with her, just a set of two keys wrapped around her wrist with a pale blue ribbon, a dagger strapped to her leg, and a curious vial, glowing faintly red. The Slayer pocketed these for herself and turned her attentions to their surroundings, considering their situation.

"Do you really think she was controlling those Soulless?" Veroh continued, trembling with fear and surprise and perhaps a little indignation. The Slayer hoped that was the case; she should be angry. "How is that even possible? Why would she do such a thing?"

"We should head back," the Slayer decided, rising up and cocking her head back in the direction they came, nudging one of the Soulless bodies out of her way with her foot as she headed back in a quick pace. It took Veroh a second, but she swiftly followed after her. "Did you truly know nothing about this? You were one of the Baroness's head assistants, weren't you? Did you have any idea what was going on here?"

"I haven't a clue," Veroh gushed, her wide and trembling eyes speaking more truth than anything else. "I can't even believe any of this! What are we going to do?"

"Right now? We head back to the throne room, see if the Captain and his soldiers are still alive. If they are, then we make a plan from there. If they aren't, then we have no choice but to fight our way out of here. If there are more Soulless throughout the fortress, then there will be no hope left for the people of Paravelle, and we must think of saving ourselves."

As they jogged down the hallway, the Slayer glanced to Veroh sideways. "Feel free to share anything that happened," she prompted; if they weren't going to move quickly, perhaps she could at least learn a thing or two about their situation. "What happened that lead you to the moment where I came in?"

"I thought I had heard something strange," Veroh said, slowly, cautiously, as if trying to make sense of her own actions as well. "So I got up to investigate what it might be."

"And?" The Slayer jumped at the chance for more information. "Yes? And then what?"

Veroh struggled, both with her words and her ability to keep up with the Slayer's determined pace. "And then....then I opened my door, and I saw them attacking the guards. I...I quickly shut it, hoping they didn't see me, but they heard me, oh, gods, they heard me, and then they tried to get in. I could hear them pounding on the door, scraping at it with their claws, trying to figure out how to get through to me. For all I know they're still there, pawing away, moaning for blood. They don't know when to stop."

Veroh stopped, a small, tormented groan slipping out of her. "And then?" the Slayer pushed, urging the young woman on.

"My next thought was of the Baron and his wife," she said. "There's a secret passage linking my room to theirs, for emergencies just like this, but I had no idea...when I got to their chamber...I would have never expected...

"What, Veroh?" she nudged her again, feeling that she was losing Veroh to the terror of her recent memories. She had to pull her back to the present, keep her from sinking under the heaviness of the situation. "What did you find when you got there?"

Veroh drew in a shaky breath, sagging a little as though her legs couldn't support her weight any more. "They were already there, the Soulless. A dozen of them, all clamoring over the bed, fighting over what few scraps of the Baron remained. And she was there, too. I didn't think anything of it; I thought maybe she was just keeping still and quiet to save herself, and I remember feeling so relieved to see her."

Another groan escaped her, as hindsight took its toll and colored her recollection in a new light. "When she saw me, she had the strangest look in her eyes. I thought it was relief, but now I'm not so sure. She gestured to me, waving me over to her, putting a finger to her lips to keep me quiet, and I edged around the perimeter of the room to reach her. There, she took my hand and held it so tight, like a death grip, and we slipped out together. Here I thought the Soulless were just distracted with the Baron; they were making quite the feast out of him, but, do you think…? You don't suppose that…?"

She couldn't get the words out, so the Slayer provided them. "She was controlling them, too?" she said. "Very likely. The Baron was a very ample man, this is true, but no matter how much a man may offer, Soulless will always go for fresher meat if it's there."

"By the stars." Veroh sounded as though she was going to be sick. "So, when I came into their bedroom, she was just standing there, watching them do that to her husband."

With that realization, the two of them reached the throne room, and Veroh's disgust reached a breaking point as they viewed the aftermath of the carnage. She hung back, using the doorframe to support her as she vomited, all the stress and terror and exhaustion catching up with her and flowing out of her. The Slayer tried to ignore the sounds of her retching, tried to ignore the rich scent of decay mingled with the warm vomit behind her. She tried to take in the scene, assess what had happened. While most of the bodies strewn about were Soulless, the Slayer noticed a few glossy stares of untainted men looking up from their deathbeds, too. She set to finding survivors, though she expected none.

"Captain!" she shouted, turning over a body that faced down to see if it was the brave young soldier.

"Here." A voice lifted up, as a figure limped out of the shadows. His broad shoulders were slumped, his helmet lost. "I'm here."

Behind her, Veroh released a shaky breath. "Gods, are you alright? Where is everyone? Are they--"

She couldn't say it. Looking around the room, she knew it to be true. At her feet, something groaned, but a sword quickly put whatever it was, man or Soulless, out of its misery.

"I...I think I'm the only one left," he muttered, blinking those dark eyes at the massacre surrounding them. Even with the blood and gore streaking down his face, he maintained an odd, unadulterated innocence. He may have shown excellent presence in the midst of battle, but now that it was over, his inexperience was bursting through. "What...Where's the Baroness?"

"She's dead," Veroh's lost, quiet voice answered. "The Baroness is dead. She was behind all of this, the whole thing."

He stared at her, as though he could not comprehend the words that she spoke. "What do you mean?"

As Veroh told the Captain of the Guard the story, the Slayer moved forward through the bodies to ensure that they were all destroyed, that they were now safe. Several quiet groans called for a heavy hand in decapitation, methodical mutilation as she had done in so many other killing fields. While Paravelle was surely lost, it was the least she could do to ensure that her fallen soldiers did not return, raising up as Soulless themselves. It was almost a mindless task, after a while, but a sudden scream of terror lifted up from the mass of bodies, captivating their attention, stopping her sword.

At first, the shout was wordless, born from panic, but as the young man pulled himself up and defended himself with raised arms, coherency gained footing.

"Stop! Please! Don't kill me!"

She stayed her weapon, staring down at the blood splattered man cowering among the corpses. He wore bits and pieces of the armor of the Paravelle guards, which seemed to have been donned in haste. She scanned him carefully for signs of disease or death, but found none. She looked at him expectantly.

Realizing that his end was not imminent, the man let out a braying, hysterical laugh that quickly took a turn toward sobbing. He pitched himself forward, wrapping his arms around her legs, hugging them tight. "Thank the gods!" he proclaimed, as she fought against the urge to be disgusted, remembering the Baroness's pleas. But one thing easily separated this man from that woman: this man's tears were utterly sincere. "Thank you! I thought I was dead for sure! Thank you! You've saved me! You've saved us all!"

With a grim look around the room, she shook her head. "I haven't managed to save anyone," she said, "and I trust the Soulless are still ravaging other parts of Paravelle, too. Who are you? Can you fight?"

"Y-yes," he stammered, his wide blue eyes regarding her pleadingly as he looked up. "Yes, of course. I'm Kyle. Kyle of the--"

"The Third Division of the Paravelle Guard," the Captain interjected, a disapproving frown on his face. "To your feet, soldier, before you disgrace your division further with this untoward and unrefined display of grovelling."

"Not much left to disgrace," the Slayer muttered. "But come on. To your feet, as he says. If the place is truly overrun, we need every sword we can get. Veroh, can you fight?"

A long silence followed, but her voice had resolve behind its shakiness when she answered. "If I must."

"And you must," she said firmly. "Let's go."

It was a bit of a misfit group, it was true, but she and the Captain were strong fighters and could carry them through any encounter. Their skills prepared them for battle, but nothing could prepare them for the carnage that had befallen Paravelle. As they left the throne room, it seemed they couldn't take a single turn without encountering another huddle of Soulless closing in on a helpless victim, as the doors no longer held them back. As if nothing held them back any more, now that the Baroness was dead and no longer controlling them. A chill raced up the Slayer's spine, considering the meaning behind that, wondering if she had acted to hastily and should have kept the woman alive. It was too late now, just as it was too late for Paravelle. The Slayer had witnessed massacres before, never before had she seen people so utterly unprepared for what would become of them.

"Paravelle is lost," she murmured, staring at another room filled with the dead, watching as more Soulless started stumbling toward her. Completely, utterly lost.

CHAPTER EIGHT

The main gates of Paravelle were just as effective at keeping people inside during a crisis as they were at keeping people out. It didn't take long for the small group to discover that the entire castle had been overrun, and the people of the city were falling fast to the Soulless hordes. There was simply no escape in sight. The pile of torn apart bodies in front of the doors was almost as high as the doors themselves, and, every time they turned a corner, it seemed that more Soulless waited for them, growing bored with the bodies they had been so eager to tear into.

While they had yet to find a viable escape route, they had managed to find four other survivors, a young man with a bloody sword who had managed so far to defend the pretty young woman all but clinging to his back, and two faces already familiar. Veroh was nearly bursting with relief to find her brother and Thom working their way through the Soulless, clinging to her sibling as the story bubbled out of her. The Slayer wished there had been more, but then the effort of escaping would have grown in difficulty with added survivors. Thankfully, Veroh's brother, who had worked on missions to the villages in the foothills, knew of another way out of the castle, a passage that very few were privy to, a service tunnel that went deep underneath the mountains. Through these tunnels, the hunting parties and recon missions would return, through a maze of cellars and hallways where they brought in their fresh kills and vegetables from the surrounding farms.

At first, the new plan see med brilliant. Slipping through a mostly hidden door, they found the tunnels to be quiet and empty. They were able to secure food and supplies from the larders, which would help for the long flight into the wilderness. For a while, it even seemed as though they had avoided the plague of Soulless toiling over them, until they eventually heard a soft moan echoing in the dark hallways. It seemed the supply rooms had been only a brief respite, as, the further down they went, the number of Soulless increased again. Thankfully, Aron, the young man they'd found, made up for Kyle's questionable sword work and Veroh continued to prove better than the Slayer had expected. Thom was still spry with his cane, hardly letting his wooden leg or his eyepatch slow him down. Perhaps they should have backed out, found another way, but the Slayer felt a need to keep pressing on. It would be foolish to turn back when nothing but death awaited them the way they came.

The Slayer was starting to wonder just how long this labyrinth went on, when they turned the corner and descended into a subterranean nightmare. At first, the change was subtle. The smooth stone of the hallways made way for natural crags and rocks, the width of the passageways no longer consistent and uniform. "I think we may have made a wrong turn," Veroh's brother noted darkly, his eyes scanning the walls as his sister lit the way with a sputtering torch. "None of this looks familiar."

"What's that?" Janessa, the other young woman to have joined them, pointed over Aron's shoulder to the faint glow that seemed to be oozing out from around a corner in front of them. The light wasn't the only thing that seemed to ooze into the darkness; the Slayer could have sworn she felt something in the air, a palpable feeling of danger, as she often did when she sensed trouble. A few Soulless stumbled forward from around the corner, targeting the small group as soon as they saw them, and, by now, the group was able to deal with them swiftly. They pressed on, eager to find the source of the glow, though it filled the air with apprehension. The Slayer didn't get her hopes up; it was too strange to be the glow of the outside.

In all her years she had never seen something so gruesome and terrifying as what waited for them in that deep subterranean chamber underneath the city. As they turned the corner, they found the source of the strange soft glow to be a great pit in the ground, as wide as one of the great chambers in the fortress above. Though the source of the light itself was unknown, they had undeniably found the source for all those Soulless leaking up into Paravelle. Reaching and grasping for the flesh that would never satisfy their ravenous cravings, the creatures managed to claw their way out from the depths of the mysterious pit, sometimes fighting against each other to make headway and stumble toward the Slayer and her party. Where did this glowing cesspool lead? How could there still be so many Soulless crawling out from it when they had already encountered so many? But they kept coming, with no sign of stopping, and the Slayer didn't have time to answer such questions. Once more, she prepared to fight, a sick stone settling in her stomach.

"What is this?" the Captain of the Guard breathed in astonishment, gawking for a fearful moment before he came back around to his senses.

"It's a pit!" Kyle gasped. "And it's filled with them! Is this where they're all coming from?

A Soulless's pitiful groan seemed to answer him, reaching out to snag his arm, but Kyle danced back and sliced it off. Aron rushed forward to aid his fellow soldier, but he had to move quickly, as there were more coming, and he had to protect Janessa as well. "There has to be dozens of them!"

"Or hundreds," the Slayer murmured. "Quickly! Someone find an exit, or we have to go back! There's no way we can kill them all!"

It was a grave understatement, for as soon as she cut down one, it seemed two more took their place. They tried edging back to the way they came, but, somehow, they had gotten in the center of the swarm, and their path was hardly clear. She cursed under her breath. "Veroh!" she called out. "Janessa! Do either of you see another exit?"

At this point, the frail Janessa was a mess of tears, cowering toward the middle of their circle and useless to her, but she had come to expect more from Veroh. She looked up to find the other girl, fearing the worst, and finding her standing stock still while Thom and the Captain sliced down Soulless around her. "Veroh!"

Veroh was trembling, her eyes locked on a form staggering out of the pit, a crooked Soulless with ribs poking out from underneath a few tattered scraps of clothes still hanging loosely from a decaying body. Those eyes were wide and filled with terror...and recognition.

"Papa?" she breathed out, barely a whisper, but the Slayer caught it as she moved forward quickly. The Soulless had let out a guttural groan, lifting its arms to reach out for Veroh and Veroh, in her dazed state, had almost lifted up her arms as if to receive the creature in an embrace. The Slayer made it just in time, her sword cleaving through the body just as it staggered forward, mouth open, teeth ready to sink into Veroh's flesh.

"No." A shaky breath left her. "No! That was my father, that was...but that's impossible. They destroyed his body. They said they had incinerated..."

"Over here!" Kyle voice lifted up over the mess of groaning Soulless, from the far wall where a small crack provided a door to their freedom. "There's another passageway over here!"

Veroh's brother sidled up to them, taking his sister by the arm and trying to push her forward, freeing the Slayer from ensuring that everyone else had a clear path to Kyle's discovery. "Come on, Veroh," he said. "We have to keep going, come on."

"But did you see?" she stammered. "Didn't you see? That was Papa; Papa was here."

"Yes, I know," he said, his voice cracking with despair and confusion. "I saw him, too, Veroh, but we musn't—"

The Slayer was ready to check out of the conversation when Veroh let out a horrified scream; she turned her head just in time to see a Soulless grab Veroh's brother's shoulders and bite into his neck, growling as the teeth sunk into his flesh, covering his sister with spurts of his blood. Another Soulless joined in on the easy prey, and a third, and more would be there soon, drawn in by the fresh scent of blood and Veroh's desperate screams. The Slayer reached out to grab her arm, using all her strength to pull the young woman away before she met the same fate as her brother. And, apparently, her father, too.

"Come on!" the Slayer shouted.

"There are too many of them!" Aron wailed in dismay, though he did not cease to fight, one arm slung out to protect Janessa while the other worked furiously to hack off the limbs trying to grab her.

"Just keep going!" the Captain ordered. "We can make it!"

There were too many of them, even by the Slayer's experience, and the worst part was that they just kept coming. A strangled gasp from Janessa told her that she, too, recognized one of the grim faces in the ravenous horde, as did a muttered curse from Thom. A picture started to form in her head, one that made her stomach clench tightly. She couldn't focus on the implications right now, though. The Soulless continued to spew forth from the Pit, unceasingly, boiling over like a pot left on for too long.

"What if they follow us?" cried Kyle.

"Then we keep fighting," the Slayer responded.

They did not follow them, though, not many of them, at least. As soon as they successfully slipped into the dark shadow of the tunnel, it was as though a switch turned off. Perhaps there were too many of them; they confused themselves in the jumble and didn't realize where the humans had gone. A few shambled after them, but they were quickly dispatched. The crack in the wall had been too narrow for most of them to easily move through, especially in the hacked-apart state the group had left them in.

A few moans mingled with their heavy breathing and Janessa's gentle sobs, but the new passageway felt strangely silent and muffled. "Let's keep going," the Slayer said, yanking her sword from the skull of their latest attacker and wiping the gore from the blade. She felt around for the wall and started heading in the opposite direction of the pit. "They might eventually trickle down here, but I'd rather be well out of their way when they do. We need to get out of these tunnels, out to the surface, and then we'll figure out what to do."

"Those Soulless back there," Janessa babbled. "Did you see them? I knew some of them. One of them...my old friend...she died of a sickness when we were—"

"Shhh." Thom's voice gently reached out like a calming embrace. "Yes, I...I noticed it, too. Best not think about it right now, though, lass. Best just focus on getting out of this nightmare."

"And my brother," Veroh softly murmured, after which they all fell into a somber silence. The tunnel was dark and treacherous, but the Captain of the Guard took the lead and forged the trail with skill. Just when the exhaustion and the terror of their situation had time to settle into their brains and get cozy, they turned a corner to find the blinding light of an opening out into the world.

"There!" Janessa cried out, dried out from her tears and wilting with relief. She leaned against Aron for support, his arm slung over her shoulders. "We've made it!"

"Allow the Captain and myself to step out first," the Slayer warned, regaining her sword. She was tired, too, but it was not over yet. "To make sure the coast is clear. When you hear us call, Aron, bring Janessa, and I want Kyle and Veroh to make sure we weren't followed before we proceed any further. It'll likely be rocky terrain up there, very difficult, and probably dangerous, so we must continue with caution."

It was safe outside the opening in the side of the mountain, much lower than the Slayer would have expected. They were greeted by a bright morning sun, the day approaching swift and warm. A road, flat and broad enough for a single cart or carriage, stretched in front of them, heading up into the mountains behind them. The area, though littered with outcroppings that so often collected mindless, shambling Soulless, was clear, and the Slayer looked back to marvel at the distance the underground tunnels seemed to take them. One could barely see Paravelle hidden in the mountains anymore. Just how far had they gone in those dark, twisting passageways?

"If there's a road," the Slayer observed, "we can't be too far from a village."

One look at her party, though, ragged and torn and lamenting the loss of their entire world, and she knew they couldn't go on. Quietly, she cursed under her breath, trying not to think of how she herself could go on for days if she had to. These refugees were not used to travelling such long distances, pushing themselves to the very brink of their being. She watched as Veroh, trying to brush away the tears that had been gathering in her eyes, stumbled over her own two feet and dropped her sword. Kyle's head dipped as he stood, eyelid heavy, nearly falling asleep. Thom started hacking with a terrible cough, depending more now on his cane than he had the entire voyage thus far.

"Kyle, Veroh," she said. "Any sign of Soulless following us?"

The soldier shook his head. "None," he said. "If any made it through that crack, we must have lost them along the way."

"Good," she nodded. "We rest, then, before we continue on. It's been a long night, and we should take a moment to make sure no one was bitten, to perhaps get a little bit of rest before we move on. Who knows how long until the next village? We'll take watches, though, to make sure no one is coming. This little cave is probably one of the best hidden spots we'll find for miles, I'd guess. We'd better take advantage of it."

Her plan inspired no argument, only murmurs of agreement and relief. They moved back into the cavern behind the small crevice in the rocks, grateful for the few supplies they were able to procure as they fled. As the Slayer set to starting a fire with Thom's help, Kyle and the Captain of the Guard set to discussing rations and a meal, while Janessa and Aron fell asleep as soon as a blanket had been spread out.

Veroh sat on the other side of their small fire, her knees tucked up to her chest, staring into the flames. "You should rest, too," the Slayer said, looking up and taking in that cold, stony face.

"I don' think I could sleep if I tried," she said quietly. When she lifted her eyes to catch the Slayer's, they were haunted and distant. "I feel the desire to know what has happened just now, but, at the same time, I don't think I want to know. Those weren't just Soulless down there. Those were the reanimated corpses of the people we knew, that died in Paravelle, that were supposedly taken care of. How long have they been down there? Why would they attack? And the Baroness! Why did you kill her? There's all the questions, and she's the only one who would know the answers."

For a brief moment, the Slayer felt as though she didn't owe Veroh anything, certainly not an explanation. They had escaped, and that was all that should better. But she also knew that tension between them was no way to begin this strange new journey. "We would not have been able to get out of there as long as she was alive," she said. "I don't know what she was doing, or how she was doing it, but no one will ever suffer at her hands again. There might still be someone who can help us, though. In the morning, I'm setting off to find the Queen. If anything, she needs to know what happened here, and what should be done. If anything."

Again, the dismal silence settled over the group, Veroh's eyes dropping again to the flames. After a moment, she spoke again. "And do you know what the worst thing about all of this is?" she asked. "We were supposed to be safe there. That was supposed to be the start of a new era. Now it's gone, just like that, just when I was starting to feel hope again. And we don't even know why! Why now? Why would she do such a thing, after everything she and Paravelle had ever worked for?"

"That's just it, though," Kyle offered, face twisting in a disgusted grimace. "We'll probably never know the answers to those questions, even if the Baroness waltzed right down that tunnel as a bloody damn Soulless herself."

"But we can try," the Captain said, much softer, but with his gentle voice firm with faith. "We can try to figure this out, see what the Queen has to say, just as the Slayer says. She's helped us before; she can help us again. This doesn't have to be the end; perhaps it's only the beginning."

CHAPTER NINE

The Slayer wanted to wait until the next morning before they left, not wanting to be left to scramble in the dark on unfamiliar terrain, and it proved to be easier than she'd have expected. Exhaustion took the lot of them, finding easy sleep where she could find little, even when it was her turn to rest. She tried to figure out what her next step should be, and she reached the same conclusion every time. Find the Queen. Tell her about what happened. Then it would be out of her hands and she'd return to what she'd always done, roaming the earth in search of Soulless, ones she could destroy, unlike the mess that now filled Paravelle to the brim.

Once the sun had risen again on the world, it didn't take the small party long to find a village, nestled down the road as the mountains smoothed out into foothills. It must have been one of the finer settlements the Slayer had seen in her journeys, clearly having benefitted from its relationship with Paravelle. Probably not much longer, she realized grimly, wondering how long it would take for the Soulless to get past those thick walls and start tearing down the mountain. Would this village be able to defend itself, or had it been lured into a sense of security, as had those in the fortress, so that they would stand no chance when all hell broke loose?

As they drifted down the dusty main street, the place was empty, though she could feel eyes watching from the shuttered windows. She couldn't blame them for being cautious; that caution was likely the reason they were in such good shape. The small, ragged band from the mountains didn't encounter another soul until they reached the commons at the center of the village. There, three young women were drawing water from the large stone well, a young man was grazing two small lambs on the surprisingly well-manicured grass, and an old beggar was sleeping face down in his dirty robes beneath a twisted, gnarled tree with very few leaves. Quiet, normal things taken for granted during moments of peace.

The women at the well noticed them first, casting a wary eye about them and the swords hanging from their belts. They clustered together for protection, the tallest of them in the middle. She spared a glance toward the shepherd, who acknowledged the newcomers dully, as if he couldn't be bothered with them when he had his two sheep to watch. The tall young woman gave a grunt of annoyance, then cocked her chin to the Slayer.

"Who're you, then?" she asked. "Why are you all covered in blood? You're not about to bring Soulless in on us, are you? If you are, you should let us know so's we can prepare!"

The mousy girl to her left piped up, pointing an accusing finger at them. "We haven't been attacked in years, you know, and we'd like to keep it that way, so if you're being followed, you'd best turn right around and find a different village to doom!"

"We aren't being followed," the Slayer informed her, scowling a little at being berated by someone with a voice as grating as the mousey one's.

"I take it your safety has been much in part to help from Paravelle?" the Captain of the Guard asked, his voice cool, his brow quirked as he considered the three women. They seemed to soften a little at his appearance, the round one on the right batting her eyes a little as she smiled.

"Well, yes," the tall one said. "In part. We send them food, they send us soldiers." A thought seemed to strike her, and she swallowed down the hard lump of an idea. "You're not from Paravelle, are you? Refugees, right, from the West, seeking the city?"

Sadly, the Captain shook his head. "Refugees, yes," he said, "but we're fleeing from the city rather than looking to enter it. I'm the Captain of the Guard of Paravelle. Let me assure you, there are no Soulless following us as of yet, but I promise you, there is trouble, a great deal of it, on its way. We must speak with the lord of your village, and we must warn any capable warrior you have to be prepared. This village...nay, the whole world!...is in great danger."

The words seemed to flow right over their heads. They merely stared at the Captain as if thunderstruck or smitten, their eyes searching over him as though they didn't know whether to focus on the power of the emblem across his armor or the allure of his soft and gentle eyes.

"You can't be the Captain of the Guard," the mousey girl said with firm conviction. "You're much too young!"

"And handsome!" added the round girl on the right.

The shepherd, finally drawn over by the commotion, took one look at the strangers in their midst and spit on the ground. "Captain of the Guard?" he sneered. "Says who? I could say I'm Captain of the Guard until my face is blue, but that don't make it true, do it?"

"He is who he says he is," the Slayer said. "I will gladly vouch for that. And if you do not recognize me either, then perhaps you will recognize my sword!" She drew it out quickly, lifting it in the air before driving it down to stand in the parched grass. "That sword as tasted the blood of more Soulless than you've ever seen in your short life. Something terrible has happened to Paravelle, and we must take action immediately. They have been overrun by Soulless. It is hopeless for them now, but there may still be hope for others, including everyone here."

A stunned silence followed her speech, eyes drifting between her and her sword. Met with only her angry glare, they could only chuckle nervously. "Pull the other one," one of the women said cautiously. "It's got bells on it."

"Don't you fools listen?" Aron stepped forward, shaking with fury. "She speaks the truth! We were all there. We owe our lives to her, and you will, too!"

Veroh spoke up next, her voice wavering, barely strong enough to support her words, but she pushed on. "The Baroness has betrayed us, and we've just lost so much.

Please, we must speak to whoever is in charge here. They have to know of the danger we're all in."

The old beggar beneath the tree stirred just then, lifting his face and his hat and hobbling forward on his cane. "You foolish children," he said in a reed-thin voice. "You make me almost wish the Soulless would take us over if only to get rid of your stupidity. Why would they make up such a story? Look at them; that's Soulless gore if I ever saw it, and I've seen enough to make you sick for days. That sword belongs to the Savior of the Untouched. Show some damn respect!"

A few more steps, and the old beggar was standing in front of the old man from Paravelle with a strange grin on his face. "And you, Thom, you old rat. I never thought I'd live to see you roll through here again."

Thom was slow to recognize the shabby fellow, his single eye rolling about his face for a few moments before he gasped in realization. "As I live and breathe, Asa! You're still rotting away out here? It's been decades. I didn't even recognize you!"

"Yeah," Asa chuckled, a sound deep in his throat like a death rattle. "You're a bit easier to spot with that blasted eyepatch. And what's that you got on your leg now, they turning you into a damn machine up there?"

The two men grinned at each other for a moment before they embraced, a hug full of pats and sighs and groaning limbs. When they pulled away from each other, Asa had his arm still slung over Thom's stooped shoulders. He waved a hand at the three women and the shepherd. "Never you mind these smart-talking embryos. They wouldn't recognize a

Soulless from their own mums. I'll take you to the Chief, Thom, don't you worry. You remember Ister, right? It's his grandson, if you'd believe it, he's running the place now."

Without another word, they started to lead the way with a hobbling gait, seeming not to even care if the others followed as Thom delved into the story of how he got his strange new leg. Trying not to be irritated, the Slayer yanked her sword back out of the ground, wiping it off before settling it back home on her hip and stalked after their elder guides. The Chief's hut was located back toward the foothills, elevated on the mounds, "so that he can survey all that surrounds him," said Asa. But the large wooden balcony supported by pillars of carved stone was empty when they climbed near, and two guards in light armor stood attention at the door. They eyed the group with curious suspicion, hands tightening on their weapons.

"My friends here request an audience with the Chief." Approaching the guards, Asa puffed out his chest and straightened his back as best he could, displaying some sort of authority that he clearly didn't have. He seemed like a caricature, an overly exaggerated image of an old man, almost comical, if it weren't for the fact that people didn't usually reach such an old age without doing something right. His behavior was so strange, yet somehow fascinating.

The guards didn't exactly seem impressed by the display, either. "Why should the Chief be disturbed by the friends of a drunken old beggar?" one of them asked, snorting softly, though he gave a wary look to the odd bunch accompanying Asa.

"Excuse me," the Captain stepped forward again to supplant the authority the beggar could never have. He fixed the soldiers with a glare that made them squirm slightly, their unease growing in the presence of someone they clearly feared more. "I am the Captain of the Guard of Paravelle, and I am here with the Slayer of the Soulless and the right hand assistant to the recently deceased Baroness. If being friends of a drunken old beggar does not garner us an audience with your chief, then perhaps our other credentials will. We have very important and grave information that he should receive immediately."

After a moment of hesitation, one of the soldiers lifted a fist and knocked on the door behind them. A few moments later, the door opened and a third soldier stuck out his head. A medley of whispers transpired, then the third ducked back inside and closed the door again.

"He's seeing if the Chief is available," one soldier explained.

"Available!" The calm facade that the Captain maintained cracked slightly around the edges. "What part of important and immediately did you not understand, soldier?"

Veroh placed a soft hand on his shoulder, stopping the tirade from building. When he glanced back, he seemed apologetic, but also pleading, and the Slayer felt uncomfortable, as if she was witnessing something very private. Thankfully, the moment broke when the door creaked open again.

"He's available," the third soldier said. "Follow me."

Inside, the hall was dark, lit by a few sputtering torches lining the wall on the way to a ladder leading up into the building they had seen on the hill, a tight, uncomfortable fit. It was an incredibly smart design. After all, the people in the hall were restricted to a cramped single file line, and Soulless were notoriously unable to climb anything more challenging than stairs or soft inclines. It provided the Chief tremendous protection, forcing an enemy to advance one by one, if they were able to advance at all. Not only that, but she realized with a clenching stomach, there was a good chance that, when she cleared the hatch in the ceiling after their escort, there would be swords up there waiting for her. It would be like leading lambs to slaughter.

Thankfully, it was no trap, though there was no lack of armed men ready like sentinels once they climbed through the hatch into the Chief's audience chamber. It took an effort to crawl through; Aron had to help Janessa, and Veroh aided the two old men, and all of them were extremely vulnerable in the effort. As little as she liked that feeling, she had to admire the sheer cleverness of it all. When this ordeal was over, she planned on spreading the idea to the other villages. Every little bit of protection helped.

Spacious and bright, a good portion of the chamber opened to the balcony, and the roof sloped up to a tall peak in the center, open at the top to let the fragrant smoke of the hearth at the center of the room escape. On the other side of the fire, a wooden throne on a raised platform sat and, inside that throne waited the village Chief.

She was surprised by how young he looked, even through the shroud of smoke that separated them. How long had she been doing this that so many people around her seemed so impossibly young? His smooth face seemed fairly untested, making her think he had only recently taken up the title. There was a cockiness there in his arched brow, one that tended to be beaten out of more experienced leaders, and a hardness, as though he was poised and ready to prove himself in the face of this odd occurrance.

"So the great Slayer of the Soulless has come calling to our humble hamlet." The Chief had a deep, rich voice that didn't seem to match his long, thin features, until one recognized the slightly haughty quality present in both. "I heard rumors you were bunking in Paravelle for a while. What brings you out to the lowly foothills?"

"My visit was cut short," she said, stepping around the fire so that she may face the Chief more directly. The soldiers immediately shifted, bending their knees at the ready, hands hovering over their hilts, but she paid them no mind. "I come bearing terrible, incredible news. The city of Paravelle is lost. The Baron and his wife are dead, and Soulless have overrun the place, leaving little hope for survival for anyone still trapped within those walls."

It seemed as though the Chief could not fully comprehend the words, though he definitely understood them. His smooth brow creased as he implored the Captain of the Guard. "Is this true?" he asked. "You're the Captain, aren't you? I recognize you from the few times you've come with the soldiers. Paravelle? Overrun with Soulless?"

The Captain nodded. "It's true. What's worse is that we believe the Baroness herself was behind the attacks. We found a pit, deep beneath the castle, where she had been keeping corpses. Where she got so many, I cannot say, but, she must have chosen that night to release them on us, once and for all. Luckily, we managed to escape, but we are the only ones we know of."

As the Chief continued to process their tale, the Slayer pressed on, her eyes drifting upwards, as though she could see the airship of the Queen flying by overhead just then. "I plan to take this matter to the Queen," she said. "I feel she should be warned, and perhaps she'll know what should be done about the matter. Have you seen her lately, or heard any word of where she might presently be?"

"I don't understand," the Cheif muttered. "How could the Baroness do such a thing? After all these years, she has done nothing but support us and protect us against the scourge. Why would she destroy her own kingdom like that?"

Though irritated with the Chief's slow understanding of the situation, the Slayer had to admit that she did not know the answer to that herself. "She was controlling them," she said slowly. "I think. I've seen enough Soulless to know that they're directed by one thing only: their own desire to kill and destroy. But they seemed to listen to her. She pretended to protect the few people she had with her, but the moment the tables started to turn, it became clear that she wasn't intending to protect anyone."

It felt so strange to relive those moment, playing them through her head again to understand the reasons why Veroh stepped forward, somewhat timidly, her face distorted from deep concentration.

"She may have been plotting it for some time now," she said, her hands folded before her as she had done many times before, though, this time, she played nervously with her fingers. "I've been going over it in my head, over and over and over, ever since we get out of that horrible place. I knew something was off, I always felt that she was hiding something from us, though I could never tell what. I think she was waiting for the right moment, and that moment had come. She had the Slayer of the Soulless, their greatest enemy, right there under her roof, and you refused her, didn't you? That afternoon at tea, she asked you to stay and you said no. She doesn't like to be told no."

Something cold and hard in Veroh's voice made the Slayer think that she had experienced it firsthand, and, recalling the odd intercourse in the tower, she could easily believe it. "Destroy her whole kingdom just because I wouldn't back down?" she murmured, and, as soon as she said it, she knew it to be true. "That sounds completely insane."

"It is insane," Veroh agreed. "And so was the Baroness."

"Madness," the Chief muttered. "Pure madness. If what you say is true, then you're right, we're in for some interesting times. Unfortunately, the Queen doesn't pass by here very often. It's a peaceful zone, and she has her interests in Paravelle more than the foothill villages, and you all know it has been some time since her last visit there. She could be anywhere."

"You've not heard any rumors?" the Slayer pressed. "Anything at all? There must be something."

"You'll have to travel south," he suggested. "Merchants speak of a lot of trouble there in the Southern Plains, and she tries to be close to the worst of the epidemics. Though if she hears of what's happened in Paravelle, she'll immediately set her course. I'll send forth some messengers, perhaps one in each direction, to get the word spread about this new plight."

"And we'll head south," the Slayer decided. "I cannot sit still and wait for her, so ensure that your messengers carry that news with them as well. We'll head to the City on the Lake, perhaps she will know then to meet us there, if we don't find her first."

The Chief nodded. "A fine plan," he agreed. "I shall send out my fastest riders immediately. We will keep a close watch on the mountains, for any other signs of trouble or others fortunate enough to escape as you have. I may offer space and lodging for those of you who wish to stay, though I must admit, provisions might be a little difficult. It has not been a fruitful harvest for us this year."

"Anything you can spare will be more than what we have," the Slayer said, feeling a strange weight lifted from her shoulders and a deep sense of gratitude. The Chief did not need to believe them, but he did, and was offering to help. "Thank you for your kindness."

"Strange times indeed may be ahead of us, Slayer," he said, with an odd smile on his face, which seemed not so much young anymore as it did hopeful. "We'll need all the kindness we can get."

CHAPTER TEN

The barracks where the Chief put them up was large and spacious; the Captain of the Guard explained that contingents of soldiers from Paravelle would often come down to the village to train, and the village also served as a resting place for pilgrims on their way to the walled city. The long building with rows of bunks was mostly empty at the time of their stay, which the Slayer found to be a small blessing. A group of three young men and a young, haggard looking family were the only ones there, and the news of Paravelle's fall had hit them hard. The heavily pregnant mother of the family broke into wracking sobs, inconsolable, although Aron tried to help make them feel better, while Janessa took to the grieving mother with an odd, distant look in her eyes. The three men had wanted to join the Paravelle guard, and the Captain pronounced them enlisted if they wanted to join them in finding the Queen instead.

"Are you planning to come with me, then?" the Slayer asked, cleaning her blade again and watching it glean in the faint light coming from the sconces on the wall. The two children from the family were watching her nearby, trying to look as though they weren't, their eyes round and fascinated. Their attention was something she was trying to ignore, so her weapon was receiving extra attention. On the bed next to hers, she noticed Veroh lean forward slightly, listening, as she tied the shoes provided to her by the villages. So many things had been left behind, yet they were able to regain some of their material losses from these kind strangers.

The Captain smiled, still so boyish and innocent, as shoulders straightened with pride. "What else would I do?" he said, almost blithely, a boy eager for an adventure he would otherwise be denied.

He was right, in a way. There was little else for him to do here in the village. "Who else plans to join us?" she asked, finding the prospect of company in her travels a strange one, indeed. She had very rarely had a company, except in rare occasions where she would escort groups of people between villages for safety. Still, the Captain would be an strong addition, and she found herself hoping that Veroh would also be coming along, if only because the other woman had seen what had happened first hand and could add her testimonial for the queen.

Kyle had seemed ready to bail, but the Captain apparently convinced him that he still held a duty to the Guard of Paravelle, so he would come as well, a sort of lieutenant, since it was all the Captain had left. Surely, the disapproving looks of their new soldiers convinced him out of shame, as well. Aron, quietly and reluctantly, declined, passing a glance over to Janessa still speaking softly with the pregnant mother. "She needs someone," he explained. "I should stay here with her."

Old Thom, reunited with his good friend, also elected to stay, noting that he could only go so far in his current condition, and, besides, someone had to hold down the fort, and he couldn't leave it to a young whippersnapper like Aron. The Slayer nodded as the Captain explained all this to her, and he passed a faint smile to the young woman pretending not to listen.

"So the only one left is Veroh," he mused. "What's the verdict there, I wonder?"

Turning a little red, Veroh stopped paying attention to her thrice-tied shoes and straightened her skirt around her. "I suppose it's best I join you as well," she said. "I was thinking of staying with Janessa, too, but it's pretty clear that she and Aron have worked out an agreement. I may not strengthen our swords much, but I do know that I have a little more diplomacy than I imagine a bunch of warriors would have. Perhaps I may still prove useful."

An odd sensation settled over the Slayer as the conversation regarding their plans dwindled, as they all settled in to rest before the next day, when they would depart again in what may be a long, tiresome search. It was not a feeling of togetherness and friendship that the others surely felt, with the way their eyes danced and their smiles nearly glowed. No, she was rarely a part of such feelings; instead, she felt removed from it all, an outsider looking in, no matter what part she may have played in bringing it all together. She felt a great emptiness. She felt lonely. There was Veroh and the Captain, their heads together now as they spoke in low tones. The three new soldiers were already giving Kyle a hard time as though they'd been banded together forever. Aron and Janessa, talking quickly to the rambunctious children of the travelling family, having abandoned their gawking for more interactive pursuits. Asa and Thom reminiscing and laughing together over so many years gone by. And all she had was her sword and a long trail of blood.

The Slayer stood, leaving the barracks to step into the night. A chill had settled in the air, but the sky was clear, revealing a thick blanket of stars overhead. When she shivered, it was not so much for the cold air in her lungs, but rather for all the times that the stars bore witness to the killing fields. She could hear fires and the low murmur of conversation from the homes of the village, but she listened instead for the familiar moans of the Soulless.

"May I fetch you a cloak?" The soft voice didn't startle the Slayer. She had heard the footsteps approaching, and, though it was clearly not a Soulless, her hand rested on the hilt of her sword. "Or perhaps a blanket? You may underestimate the cold, and wouldn't that give the myth tellers a field day? The great Slayer done in by a common cold."

Stopping, she turned to find the Chief standing there, flanked by two stone-faced guards holding spears. His face, by contrast, held a smile. She tilted her head slightly before affording him a nod in greeting. "What are you doing here?" she asked.

Laughing slightly, the Chief held out his arms as if to show he had nothing to hide. "I'm quite fond of a stroll in the evening," he said. "A man who may traverse his lands is better fit to rule them, don't you think? I was hoping I might catch you as well, for a private moment. Those in positions like ours can rarely seem to find such a thing, don't you agree?"

The hairs on the back of the Slayer's neck lifted, trying not to see the same pleasantness in the Chief's voice that she had found in the Baroness's appeals. "Private?" she asked. "Even with guards?"

If she had caught him in something, he had the decency to be embarrassed about it. "These are rough times," he said. "A man in my position can never be too careful. The last chief of this village met a grisly demise. I do not care to meet the same fate."

"Soulless?" she asked.

But he shook his head. "Enemies. He'd made quite a few, and it was decided that a new chief should be chosen. The duty fell upon my shoulders, though I'm sure there are many out there who wished it was someone else. Because of that, I can't be too careful. My position alone puts me in danger with the dissatisfied populous."

"Strange, isn't it?" the Slayer found herself murmuring, and she started to walk again around the outskirts of the village. The Chief joined her, his guards just a few steps behind. "That even with a much greater danger looming outside your door, you'd rather bicker and squabble with your own like fools. Even worse when those bickers and squabbles reach a death toll. If you asked me to stay, and I refused, would you then try to destroy me?"

"I might if I were mad," the Chief said lightly. "There have always been strange rumors about the Baroness, you know. Her brother is the same way, with a small kingdom down south, and you hear such strange things. Still, you have an interesting point. Do we truly turn on each other when the Soulless no longer threaten us? Perhaps it is only in our nature."

The Slayer scoffed slightly, but she decided not to put a voice to her thoughts. They disturbed her far too much, and the Chief seemed willing to let her lapse into her silence, keeping a slow and steady pace with her as they skirted the perimeter. She took to a survey of the village as they strolled in silence, a watch around to get a lay of the land and access any weak points during an attack. This was a ritual for her whenever she arrived at a new village and stayed for any amount of time. It never hurt to be prepared. There was a clean simplicity to the place, which was good. No complicated pockets or architecture that pigeonholed or trapped a person during a moment of chaos or panic. Good height on the roofs, and more buildings that seemed to take advantage of the narrow hall and ladder entrance. This village might have been fairly free of attacks lately, but the evidence was in the bones. Once upon a time, this place was a hotbed for Soulless attacks. Soon, the citizens of this little hamlet in the foothills might be truly grateful for their resourceful ancestors.

When he broke the silence, it was to tell her that it was an honor to meet her, and that he wished her the best of luck, and that he was glad he was able to provide at least a little bit of help. He nodded his farewell, and the guards escorted him back into his little hall on top of the gentle foothills, the dark shadows of the mountain looming over them. Though it remained quiet and calm, she couldn't help thinking of the harsh truth that it could be interrupted with terror and death at any moment. Weariness began to creep into her bones, but her feet kept carrying her. The villagers slept soundly or chased their troubles away in the public house. She considered slipping inside for a drink, tempted by the warm glow of their hearthfires, but she was never one for drinking. She drifted alone for several more hours until she finally returned to the barracks.

She took a moment to luxuriate in the rare opportunity to be pulled from sleep by the natural rhythms of her body and not by some approaching Soulless attack when she awoke the next morning. She couldn't linger, though. She rolled out of bed, gathering her things and redressing herself in her armor. She secured her sword with a quiet, little prayer that she might make it through another day to secure it again the next morning.

It did not take long to find the others. Morning had broken beautiful and bright, though it might have been more appropriate to call it afternoon. She winced at the bright midday sun, wondering how long she'd slept. She must have needed it if her body allowed it, but she couldn't help thinking of all those wasted hours. She followed the sound of conversation and the aroma of food to find lunchtime feast in progress on the green village commons. Plentiful but simple offerings were spread out on a few wooden tables, where her companions were gathered, breaking their fast.

The Captain lifted a cup in greeting as she approached. "Our apologies for not waking you," he said. "We figured you don't get much rest and could use whatever you could get. Chief apologized that he couldn't join us for this meal, but he has offered a cart and a horse. I figured we'd make better time on foot, and our supplies would last longer without a great beast to feed in addition to ourselves."

She looked over the breads and cheeses, dried meat and bruised fruit. There was a hearty brown stew of sorts and a mead so potent she could smell it even where she stood. The Captain and Kyle, the three new soldiers, Veroh, and a few villagers staring at her with wide, fascinated eyes were gathered around the table. She frowned for the few missing faces. "Where are Aron and Janessa? Where are the old men? Did they not care to see us off?"

"It's the most amazing thing," Veroh said, with an almost mystified expression. "We spoke with the village healer today, and he recognized signs that Janessa was with child. The midwife confirmed it! So she's been in bed all morning. And though it isn't his child, Aron hasn't left her side since. As for the old men, who knows? They've got an awful lot of catching up to do, it seems."

The news of Janessa's pregnancy hit the Slayer in a strange way, something in her gut twisting. She didn't know how to respond at first, finally struggling to put a few words together. "I shall have to congratulate Janessa before we depart," she murmured. "A new life in this world of death is truly a special thing."

"She hasn't stopped crying since she heard the news," Kyle sneered as he stabbed a knife into a block of pale yellow cheese. "Can't say I blame her. It's one thing to raise a new life in Paravelle, but out here? What's the point? The child would be better off never born."

One of the soldiers, an older, rugged one, grunted into his soup and a woman nearby shook her head. "Foolish boy," she said. "I take it you've got no children of your own, otherwise you'd know better. Most precious thing in the world. Not all of them turn out all bitter and jaded, neither. We need some little ones to become the next great slayers and guardians, don't we? Maybe even lead us out of this horrible existence. The whole world was peaceful once, they say. Perhaps it can be peaceful again."

Kyle looked as though his lunch was about to come right back up from his stomach. He was about to debate the woman on the matter, too, but Veroh smartly stepped in to change the course of the discussion. It seems already her claim of usefulness through diplomacy was proving true. "Come," she said, smiling up at the Slayer as she moved over to make space at the table, "join us. The Chief has done an excellent job providing for us. We should probably leave shortly after this meal, and get back on the road to the Southern Plains before it gets too late again."

Sitting down, the Slayer's stomach grumbled, a reminder of just how hungry she was. "A quick meal, perhaps," she said. "Then, you're right. We should be off. I'll have to say good-bye to the others first, though."

After the meal, she found Aron and Janessa in the hut of the midwife, a strong and sturdy woman with large and capable hands. The young woman was settled comfortably in a bed, surrounded by blankets and resting from all the excitement. As soon as the Slayer entered, Aron stood, releasing Janessa's hand, but the Slayer motioned for him to sit back down again. He complied, opening his mouth to speak. Once more, she stopped him, moving over to the other side of the bed.

"Please," she said. "I've only come to see how she's doing and to say goodbye. The others gave me the news. Congratulations."

Before she had even finished, Janessa broke into tears, great heaving sobs that shook her whole frail body. Aron leaned in, wrapping an arm around her shoulders. "She's still in a bit of shock," he explained. "Everything is so overwhelming right now."

The Slayer nodded as if she understood, but she didn't. Those wrenching tears just seemed like a terrible waste of energy and emotion to her. "I...I'm sorry," Janessa said through hiccupping gasps, leaning against Aron. "I just can't get my head around this, around everything. Everything's changed so much, and now I'm...and the father...and Paravelle..."

Overcome with tears, Janessa couldn't continue. Wincing slightly, the Slayer watched as Aron brought his other arm around Janessa, burying her sobs with his chest.

He looked over her tousled hair at the Slayer. "I'm sorry I can't come with you," he said. "I thought about it, that nothing could be more important than getting to the bottom of this, but I was wrong." He gently rubbed Janessa's shoulder, but it only seemed to give the sobs new life. "There are more important things. What good is defending the land if no one is defending the people?"

"How can you protect the people," she countered, "if you can't protect the land?"

His smile was sad, though oddly content. "Then I suppose it takes both kinds of people," he said, so serenely that even Janessa seemed to settle; perhaps she had merely exhausted herself. Or perhaps, strange as it seemed, she had been able to find some sort of comfort just from his presence and his reassuring embrace.

"I'm sorry," he said.

But she let him be, as much as she regretted to lose an able body. They had gained three, after all. The Slayer left the hut of the midwife, seeking Thom and finding him in a hut with a pinch-faced woman claiming to be Asa's sister. The two old men were cackling and sharing stories over some warm mugs of mead, and she couldn't blame them for wanting to remain in that happy state any more than she could blame Janessa for wanting to remain as comfortable as she could in hers. She supposed that it was good that they had found something else to keep them going, but she had to keep moving in a different way. She agreed to one mug of mead with them, a mug that seemed too small and too deep, all at once.

CHAPTER ELEVEN

Stocked up on supplies and bidding farewell to the company they kept in the foothill village, the party set out for the Southern Plains, feeling much stronger and more focused. The Slayer of the Soulless, the Captain of the Guard, and Kyle led the march, the three borrowed soldiers brought up the rear, and Veroh, easily the least experienced fighter, stayed in the middle. Their packs were heavy and full, but that didn't seem to slow them down, as they were refreshed and eager to forge ahead. Soon, though, those packs would lighten, just as their renewed energy was likely to dwindle. Hopefully, by then, they could find another settlement.

With certain indication of where the Queen could be found, the journey ahead would be long and brutal. At least the sky was overcast with clouds, protecting them from the harsh heat of the sun. The Slayer preferred silence, too much noise might attract danger, but eventually even the steady shuffling of their own feet started to grate on her nerves. To break the uncomfortable quiet, one of the new soldiers would sing, traditional ballads that his mother, a myth teller, had taught him. He had a beautiful voice, with a pitch higher than expected but soft and ethereal, and he might have been a myth teller himself if he had not been so desperately needed to pick up a sword rather than a staff.

As he finished a slow, moving song about an orphan finding his way back home, Veroh sighed almost dreamily. "You have truly missed a calling," she said. "Perhaps you should consider taking up your mother's trade when this is all over, or once your bones can't handle fighting any longer. Myth tellers do tend to live long and respected lives."

He smiled and bobbed his head gratefully for her kind words. "If only I could be so blessed to die an aged and revered man," he said, "though the appeal of a younger, glorious death is not lost on me, either. Only time will tell which path awaits me."

"Sing us another," one of his brother soldiers suggested, and he obliged, regaling them softly until the sky began to darken, and they had to consider making camp or stumbling on in the evening darkness. No one in the party found that option appealing, so a campsite within a small thicket was claimed. They determined a rotation of watches, and a small, mostly concealed fire was constructed to aid in the quieting of their rumbling bellies. The night came and went without trouble or disturbance, much to everyone's relief, and to the Slayer's unsettled suspicion.

The next day passed by much as the first, uneventful and undisturbed, as did the following night. The Slayer supposed she should be grateful for this blessing, but she couldn't help being unnerved by it. "I've never gone so long without a Soulless attack," she explained, when Veroh asked after her troubled expression. "It's as if all the Soulless in the world had been drawn into Paravelle."

"We could only be so lucky," Kyle said, but they all knew if that were the case, they had something much different than Soulless to worry about.

On the third day, feeling confident that they must be coming across a village again soon, the group set off to the march of the singing soldier's quiet and rapturous voice. He had only gotten about three lines in, though, before the Slayer halted holding up a hand to encourage the others to do the same. "Shhh," she hissed. "Listen."

They all stood still, their eyes turned expectantly toward her as she listened. "What is it?" asked Kyle, his voice harsh and impatient with a twinge of panic. "Is it Soulless?"

"It might be." The Slayer curled her hand around the hilt of her sword. "Shut your mouth and pray it's not so."

Still, a part of her hoped that it was Soulless, to settle the awful suspicion that something had gone amiss in the world while she was in Paravelle. Soon, though, the sounds became clearer, not the moaning, famished stumbling of the Soulless, but a jangling of things and a soft uniformity of movement. Another party of humans, it would seem. They held caution as tightly as they did their weapons, though, turning toward the approaching sounds.

A larger group than theirs soon crested the gentle hill, too large, making them an easy target by the Slayer's estimation. They were more ragged, their clothes worn and dirty, their backs hunched, and their cart, pulled by two tired mules, rattled to create that strange jangling noise. There were young children and old men, matronly women and boys clutching swords they were far too young to be wielding. These were survivors of an attack. She recognized their destitution right away, feeling a strange mix of relief and dismay for their plight.

The group was heading in a different direction, so she hesitated, considering just letting them pass, since they did not seem to see the Slayer and her party. But they might have information; they probably knew something that she didn't. If they had been attacked, then there was action where they had come from, and the Queen usually went to where the action was.

"Halt!" the Slayer called out to them, making her stance firm and domineering. Her steel whispered to her as she slid it from its sheath. "Stop, or we will have no choice but to attack."

"Is that really necessary?" Veroh whispered.

"Yes," she whispered back, never letting her eyes falter away from the party, which had indeed stopped. A ripple of fear and anticipation worked down the line, as they drew together for protection. "Even if we have no intention of attacking, this gives us the upper hand. They will appease us if it means their continued survival."

She lifted her voice again to carry up the sloping hill. "What say you? How do you answer my demands?"

"Answer what demands?" It took a moment, but, eventually, someone called back, with a careful but strong reply. "You've made none except to halt, and we've done that. We want no trouble. We've had enough of that already, thank you very much."

The Slayer bristled at the rebuke. "You seem rather bold," she noted, not as mildly as she would have liked, "for a drifting group of refugees."

"It is our boldness that has allowed us to survive long enough to be refugees," the same person said, a young man barely old enough for the stubble on his square chin. Despite his youth, he possessed a great sense of confidence and experience in his steady, bloodshot eyes. She took a moment to look him over, noting that he squared his shoulders and stared straight up at her as she observed him. His clothes were ragged and stained with dirt and blood; a large rusted cleaver hung at his belt. He carried a large, bulky sack over his shoulders. "Who are you?" he asked.

"We are also survivors," she said, "from the north. Have you been travelling far? We are trying to find the Queen and her currently location. Do you know anything about it?"

The young man glanced to the older woman on his left, who shrugged her shoulders. The silent question was passed around until it was clear no one knew the answer. "I'm afraid not," he said. "Sorry. We've had other things on our mind, but we haven't been on the road long. Only half a day in that direction, and you'll find our village, or what's left of it."

"You'll still likely find those bloody Soulless milling around," another voice chimed in, "if you're so feisty for a fight. We've had enough, though. We're trying to make it to Paravelle."

Surely, they knew something was wrong the moment they spoke the name of the fallen citadel, and the Slayer's party drew a collective breath. "Paravelle is no more," the Captain explained. "There's a village there, just north of here, that can take you in, but we come from the walled city, and we're fleeing the terror within. The place is overrun with Soulless."

The shock seemed to radiate from them, in their disbelieving expressions. A murmur rose up, like the buzz of a hornet's nest recently kicked. In a way, they seemed as though the news had been a swift kick to their stomachs. "Paravelle?" croaked the old lady. "Fallen? That's impossible!"

"We thought so, too," Veroh said sadly. "But we were proven horribly wrong. That is why we must find the Queen. She had to know about this incredible tragedy."

"Go to the village we speak of," the Slayer suggested. "Seek out an old man with one eye and a mechanical leg. His name is Thom, and he will explain everything, as he was there with us. We will continue on, toward your village, to make sure the monsters don't follow you there."

After a long moment, the young man nodded, glancing around to get silent confirmation from his companions. "Thank you," he said. "We'll do just that. But be careful. It was a devastating attack, and it's a surprise we managed to get out of there at all."

They found his words to be true after half a day's travel, when the sun was threatening to set on their journey once more, buildings dark against the horizon. As the Slayer was watching the sky, her foot found a bone, the length of an arm, crunching underneath her boot. A small sound of disgust left Veroh as she realized the small lumps ahead of them were actually bodies, little more than shreds of cloth and flesh clinging to bone. They could hear the sounds of a river nearby, loud enough to disguise their steps, but also to hide the shuffling sound of the Soulless as they emerged from the shadows of the village.

Somehow, suddenly, as they were distracted by the soft moans that rose from across the meadow, several of them were already there, close enough to reach them with their gnarled fingers. Someone cursed, one of the foothill soldiers, unable to move away fast enough. His wretched screams as the claws dug into him and the Soulless sunk its teeth into the tender open spot as his neck served as a warning to the others, though it was clearly too late for him.

Immediately, everyone spurred to action. The Slayer knew every second wasted was another second that these abominations lived. She swiftly set to the task of severing head, cleaving bodies in two, crushing skulls under her boots. She danced to the song of whistling steel and groans and howls, while her eyes scanned the area to determine where they were coming from and how many there might be. As was often the case, the moment one started in on its victim, the more Soulless were called over. They seemed to seep out of every corner and every hidden spot, as if they could just emerge out of thin air and never cease coming.

As accustomed as she was to fighting the Soulless by herself, it was refreshing to have others with her that could take up some of the demanding task. Their efforts were far from perfect, different styles clashing with different levels of fear and capability, but they held their own as the swarm settled in. The Soulless were flushed and full from recent feedings, making them stronger, though some were new and fresh, bodies that somehow survived with their brains still untouched, leaving them susceptible to the strange virus that turned them into these beasts.

The Soulless weren't the only ones hiding in the shadows. Encouraged by the new warriors cleaving through the invasion, many others arrived, shooting arrows from roofs or emerging from darkened doorways to put a blade through a skull when one of them struggled. Before long, what had seemed like an overwhelming horde had dwindled down to a few desperate enemies, easily disposed of. They had fought their way to the center of the village, to the middle of a grassy park scattered with bodies. The Slayer, breathing heavily, looked up to take stock of those still standing.

"Quickly," she said, gesturing vaguely, and sheathing her sword, "all of you. We have to get all the bodies we can and set them on fire. It's the only way to ensure they don't come back, unless we want to go around stabbing them all in the head."

Some of them must have been through this before; they were dragging the corpses over before she had even finished speaking. They had to make several piles, and, occasionally, a shout rose up where another Soulless had been found, but it was clear the danger had mostly passed. Besides the Slayer's own group, there were only a few other survivors left, looking haggard and tired and eager to accept whatever food the group could spare.

"Why didn't you join the others leaving this place?" the Slayer asked, after she had directed the small Guard to construct barriers for them. Night was settling in fast, and they would want a sheltered resting place if they were going to stay here. Not many of the building were sufficient anymore, but she had found one that they could fortify, flushed of Soulless and better protected than most.

The question brought a round of shrugs and half-hearted answers. Most of them, it seemed, felt they were trapped. Others wanted to stay, ride it out and wait for the Soulless to move on, and hopefully continue their lives as they had before. "But this was definitely the worst one yet," said a tired woman with a wide-eyed child still clinging to her skirts. "I'm not sure we can survive another."

"No," the Slayer said grimly. "You won't."

"I know who you are." The child moved out from behind her mother, eyes trained on her wide and imploring. "You're the Slayer of the Soulless, aren't you? That's why you could kill them. You actually came to save us."

A smile blossomed there on that grimy, dirt-matted face, and the Slayer shifted uncomfortably. "I hardly saved you," she said. "I merely delayed the inevitable. But there might be enough of you to make it north with the others. You have to get to a safer place. You'll never survive here if you stay."

"We always stay," another village said shrugged almost sheepishly. "Remain and rebuild. We are survivors here. We have been for ages."

She knew then that she would not convince them of anything, and though it made little sense to her, she was not surprised. She had seen it all over this green earth, people tied to their homes as if it held their very lifeforce, even when the lifeforce of all those around them had been destroyed by Soulless. Perhaps they were onto something, though. If they had left for Paravelle after their last attack, they would all likely be dead by now. As they were now, they shambled back to their homes, shifting through the damage to access how best to rebuild and start again.

The bodies had continued to burn throughout the night, even after a light drizzle had finally released from the clouds overhead. None of the villagers could provide positive information about the location of the Queen, but they had confirmed that the Soulless seemed to have come from the south, so that was where they set their course. A young woman had joined them, eager to lend her experience to their party and escape from her dismal situation; two children had also attempted to follow suite, lifting swords in an effort to prove their skill, but they were talked out of it by their mothers. All the Slayer could think of was how she was much younger than those wee little ones when she set off on her quest, and if, by the time Janessa's future child reached their age, it would want to do the same.

"Must we continue trodding even in this blasted rain?" Kyle grumbled after a long while, when the drizzle had developed into the making of a full-fledged storm. "It may be wiser to stop and set up camp before we're so waterlogged we can't even move."

"The rain would waterlog a camp just as easily," the Captain offered in a quiet voice.

"Soulless do not stop for droplets of rain," the Slayer said. "Neither do we."

They trudged on, with mild complaint, and great prongs of lightning began to illuminate the sky as bright as day. She scanned for signs of habitation in these sudden flashes, accompanied by great rumbling in the distance. If the Queen was up there, she would be avoiding this mighty storm for sure, so she redirected their course, in the opposite direction of the roiling clouds. Once, they could see the stark relief of figures on the eastern horizon, but whether they were human or Soulless, they never knew. They never stopped long enough to find out.

Eventually, though, they found an old road heading in the direction they were heading, and the Slayer was glad for it. It even felt a little familiar to her, though so many of these ancient roads felt the same to her. Though it had become difficult in the past centuries to maintain the long twists of roads between the cities of ancient times, faint ghosts of them still existed, broken and given over to nature. Sometimes, they would lead nowhere but mere ruins of the world gone by, but they would often provide the way to some shadow of civilization. Carefully treading to avoid the cracked bricks and twisted roots from the wild trees, they found a crumbling old outpost to provide shelter. The ground inside was damp, small pools of rainwater collecting around broken concrete and shards of old pottery and furniture, but they were safer there, tucked into the second level of the building. The floor was still sturdy and the roof barely leaked. Black marks on the floor from fires past signified that they weren't the first to take shelter there, either, and the longer she sat there against the wall, the more the Slayer remembered having used this outpost herself, long ago, meaning there may be a few settlements nearby, if they had survived in the long years since she had last been down this way.

Most of them slept, leaning against each other and giving in to their utter weariness. Kyle even snored slightly, a sound not likely to attract any Soulless, though it may sound start grating on some nerves. The Slayer seemed the least inclined to slumber, remaining awake and staring at the fire, but she was not the only one who found rest to be an elusive beast.

"Do you ever think it will ever stop?" Veroh asked softly from the other side of the fire. Over the low, dancing flames, her face was awash in shadows, highlighting her round white eyes. "All those Soulless. Do you think we'll ever be able to defeat them, or will there just always be more?"

"Probably," the Slayer said. "And we will keep fighting them for as long as we have to. I'm not sure we'd even know what to do with ourselves if they weren't there."

"Of course," Veroh's sigh carried in the gentle wind as the storm died down, "but don't you ever get tired of it? Don't you just wish it would finally end, once and for all?"

She wondered if Veroh could see her weak, exhausted smile in the darkness. It was the only response she would get, as the Slayer didn't know how else to respond. She had heard a ghost of the Baroness in those words, had seen those intense eyes boring into her again, and she wanted to get the image out of her head. She knew she couldn't be honest with Veroh. She doubted Veroh could understand that, if the Soulless ended, so did the Slayer.

CHAPTER TWELVE

As the small group of warriors travelled down the broken road for several days, thankfully with only a few signs of Soulless to slow them down, the Slayer began to feel a sense of familiarity about it, as though she had travelled this road before. She thought it was perhaps because all roads looked the same, but, no, there was that river, swollen right now from the rain, with the foundation of a bridge that used to cross it still there, stately stone wrapped with ivy and vine. If she wasn't mistaken, there would be a few villages coming up along the way, taking advantage of the fresh river water and the massive forest that sprung up and spread out great distances, so thick that no one could pass beyond. She always imagined someone hacking their way through the thick brambles and roots and trees, to either find a place with no Soulless or to find the opposite, centuries old Soulless, waiting and starving.

They could see the spires of cook fires and chimneys rising into the slowly clearing sky up ahead, but their first indication was a loud voice ordering them to stop. They obeyed easily enough; most of them lifted their hands, even, to show their innocence, and the Slayer followed the sound of the voice to the top of one of the tall trees beside the road. Inside the thick branches, there was a platform, and, on that platform, two men with bows primed and ready.

"State your name and your business," the voice said, "or suffer the consequences."

"I am the Slayer of the Soulless," she announced, lifting her chin to dare him to defy her, "and I am accompanied by survivors of Paravelle and others who have joined me on my way to find the Queen. We only seek to replenish our supplies and perhaps gather some information."

"Survivors of Paravelle?" the voice asked, though she noticed that the archers in the tree eased on their bows, if only slightly. Down the road, where the village started, a few people passing had craned their necks curiously toward them, though they then hurried about whatever business they were conducting.

"The messenger we sent must not have made it," the Slayer realized, wondering if any of the Soulless they killed on the way here had once been the young man sent out from the foothills. "Paravelle has been overtaken by Soulless. We barely escaped from the nightmare ourselves, and we wish to inform the Queen and figure out what can be done. Have you heard anything of her location?"

Whispering from the trees like a gentle breeze through the leaves, the soldiers seemed to be discussing this new information. "To the west," a new voice responded. "Isn't she supposed to be by the City on the Lake soon? We're promised a supply of their glassworks in a few weeks' time."

"Thank you," the Slayer ducked her head in gratitude. "And as for our own supplies?"

Lowering their weapons, the archers hesitated until one of them gestured to bring forth a pair of soldiers from behind another tree, while the other spoke their instructions. "We'll see what we can do," he said. "We'll have you meet with Lord Gizak. He will want to know about Paravelle, if what you speak is true."

As they followed the soldiers in through the streets of their village, the Slayer was impressed by how well kept it was. She took in the buildings of stone and brick, suggesting that they did not need to rebuild often, as well as the hale and hearty look to the people around her.. As she considered this, Veroh leaned in close, whispering in her ear.

"Lord Gizak is the Baroness's brother," she said, quietly so only the Slayer could hear. "I can't believe we've made it this far south already, but that might be why he'll be interested in what happened. We might want to proceed with caution."

Veroh's whispering caught the attention of one of the guards, turning his head and giving her a hard look. She met it with a faint smile, bobbing her head. "I was just telling the Slayer about Lord Gizak," she explained. "Or what little I do know. I worked in the Baroness's court, you see."

Though the suspicion didn't leave, the soldier seemed satisfied with that as an answer for now, and continued leading them on their way. The more they walked through the village, most of it built out of some already existing ruin of the world gone by, the more unsettled she began to feel. Perhaps it was just her natural tendency to be suspicious of anything too pristine, but something did not seem right here.

"How long has it been since this place has seen an attack?" she finally asked, no longer able to curb her astonishment. There was even a small patch of a garden in the center courtyard, sprouting a few yellow squashes and pale red tomatoes, where other attempts to grow produce seemed to quickly be trampled by the shambling, careless footsteps of Soulless.

"Several weeks now," the soldier said. "Practically a month, and, even then, it was a small batch, barely a dozen. Most of the settlements in the surrounding areas seem to absorb the majority of the attacks, and our fighters are well trained in range weapons, so they can usually stop the Soulless before they get too close. We send out rangers, too, to clear the area before anything gets too close. I'm surprised you didn't encounter any on your way here. Perhaps they've been slacking off."

"Perhaps," the Slayer muttered mildly, and the conversation died down as they approached Lord Gizak's manor. It was a great stone building of three stories, a marvel of architecture rarely seen, though she remembered seeing it before, the last time she passed through. It was in much better condition now, clearly taken care of, though some of it still showed signs of its previous state of ruin. So few buildings of this size remained from the time of the ancients; one wing had been destroyed, most of the walls crumbling down, though some archways for doors still stood incongruously, while a wild garden sprouted around them. Someone had tended to it slightly to create paths through the trees and shrubs, an effort to tame nature into something with a hint of orderliness. Through the foliage, the Slayer could see a young woman watching them from where she sat on a low wall like a bench, two children playing at her feet. She never took her eyes off the party until the view of the garden was obscured when they stepped up to the doors.

Groaning in protest, the large oak doors were opened and the guide gestured them inside. The Slayer went first, blinded for a moment by the darkness within, but her eyes eventually adjusted. Light streamed in through the windows behind them, dusty motes settling on the ancient furniture inside. They were marvels of a long ago past, slightly broken but set about with the reverence of a collector. It felt like stepping through a mausoleum, a grim testament to a world long gone, some of the strange objects so mysterious that one could only guess at their actual use. Other items, chairs, desks, bookshelves stuffed with odd little knick-knacks and almost-crumbling books, were much more familiar, but still held the spell of ages in their worn curves and cushions.

Back at the far end of the room was another door, flanked by guards standing so still that at first she thought they had been part of the decor, wooden statues in old fashioned armor. "Please inform Lord Gizak that he has guests," their guide said. "See if he's available to receive them. They say it's important."

One guard left, armor creaking. The other tightened his grip on his spear, narrowing his eyes at the group.

"Please don't touch anything," he snapped, and Kyle, looking nonplussed, retracted his hand from the nearby table littered with random objects. "You are currently in the most well-preserved ruin of the ancient world. Nowhere else will you find such a collection. Lord Gizak would very much like to keep it so, which means keeping your filthy paws off the relics."

So they stood there in silence, feeling oddly new and fresh amid all the ancient and decrepit artifacts, even in their worn and battered travelling state. From a looming shelf, glassy eyes from the veined faces of porcelain dolls watched them, blank and lifeless. Some of the books seemed fused into their shelves with dust and grime; they seemed so old and weathered that, were they to be opened, the pages inside would crumble to ash. There was something surreal and terrible about the place, like time had stopped and then forgotten to start up again. It sent a shiver up the Slayer's spine, and she turned away, staring at the soldiers instead, who were fresh and flesh, something real and current.

The guard finally returned, looking as distasteful as before. "They may enter the main hall," he said, "but the Lord will be a few moments. He is finishing up a game of chess with his son."

Chess! The Slayer felt a jolt of surprise, an oddly pleasant one, to think that someone else might know the ancient game. She herself had been taught at a much younger age by a mysterious mountain hermit, who contributed to years of her training. She had yet to encounter another person familiar with the game after concluding her studies with the old man, though it was possible she didn't realize it. Games were hardly something she had time for.

Following the guard through the door, they entered a great audience chamber constructed up around the old ruins of the manor. Giant pillars held up the low ceiling and a long runner led down the hall to a raised stone platform with five wooden thrones on top, two large, two small, and one somewhere in between. All five were currently empty, though each pocket of space between the pillars held a guard. To the left side, an astonishing number of windows from the old structure were still intact, looking out into the bramble of a garden she had seen earlier. Some vines had started to creep in through the cracks in the wall, reaching up the wall and across the ceiling, and she imagined the glossy green ivy leaves eventually overtaking the entire room. Somewhere in the shadow of the sylvan chamber, the soft and gentle hooting of a bird emerged, creating a strange juxtaposition between the natural world and the created one. The Slayer's party gathered in a small cluster before the empty thrones, the unwavering eyes of the silent guards locked upon them.

"This place is incredible," the Captain of the Guard breathed out, barely a whisper, into the unsettling stillness. Though his shoulders were tense and ready should any of the guards move, he allowed himself to marvel at the crawling ivy, the strong pillars, the shining glass windows.

"Incredibly creepy, if you ask me," Kyle added.

"No one did," remarked one of the foothill soldiers with a faint, lopsided grin that he shared easily with his friends.

Though they had that brief moment, silence settled uncomfortably over them, as they continued to wait with no sign of Lord Gizak. The Slayer found herself growing restless, thinking of all the time they were wasting, her eyes traveling up to the ceiling and imagining the Queen passing overhead as they squandered away, waiting for some privileged lord to finish his ancient and irrelevant game of war.

"How much longer must we stand here?"   Kyle murmured, for once voicing everyone else's thoughts. "This is ridiculous."

"My, such a lack of patience." A smooth female voice seemed to fill the chamber, the acoustics amplifying it, meaning no one could pinpoint the source right away. Eventually, though, a slim woman emerged from the shadows of the pillars, carefully stepping up onto the dais with two small children in tow. The Slayer recognized her as the woman in the garden. She stood facing them, her hands folded demurely in front of her and the children standing just a bit behind her with admirable obedience. "You'll set a poor example for the impressionable minds of my son and daughter. Don't worry, my husband will be here soon."

With that, she turned, so smooth it felt like she was moving in water, and she took a seat on one of the center thrones. The children perched themselves on the smaller ones and eyed the party with poorly hidden excitement and curiosity. The woman lifted her hand, a small nut held in her palm, and she let out a faint whistle, calling forth the bird heard earlier, a great snowy-grey owl that swept down from the shadows with a majestic swoop. It plucked the nut from the woman's hand neatly, then settled on the back of her throne, ruffling its feathers and hooting softly. It seemed as though the owl had promptly gone to sleep, but the bird brought up a sudden, sharp feeling in the Slayer's nerves, a sudden urge to grab it, break its neck, tear it apart. She shook her head fiercely to try to dislodge the violent desire, but it lingered, even as she tried to focus again on the matter at hand.

"Maybe we won't have to wait long," the Slayer said. "We've only come to inform Lord Gizak of some terrible news, and then we have to be off. Perhaps you could fetch him for us, tell him that we really must be on our way?"

Lady Gizak held a strange look on her face, slightly disdainful as she lifted her chin as though to look down on them better. "You're the one they call the Slayer of the Soulless, aren't you?" she asked, something in her voice grating on the nerves that the owl had already somehow shredded. A strong dislike grew in the bit of her stomach, the loftiness reminding the Slayer far too much of the Baroness.

"That is what they call me, yes."

"And what would the Slayer of the Soulless want with my husband?" she asked. "I'm sure you must have noticed that we have no use for your sword here; we have our scourges well under control. Aren't you best off somewhere unable to defend itself?"

Prying her gnashing teeth apart, the Slayer fought to keep her anger in check. "Of course I am," she said. "That is why I can't stand to wait here a moment longer just to tell your husband the news that Paravelle has fallen!   My companion here thought he should know that his sister is dead, and a trai—"

"—a tragedy," Veroh burst in, stepping forward with her voice rising over the Slayer's.   She cleared her throat and wrangled the situation out of the territory the Slayer's rage had almost lead it into.

"A great tragedy has occurred, my lady.   We thought he should know before we move on to also inform the Queen."

Her brow creased with confusion, Lady Gizak glanced between the two of them to try to discern which to listen to. "Fallen?" she asked.   "But what do you mean?"

There were footsteps coming from the stairwell behind the thrones, however, and Lady Gizak stood, turning her head toward the sound.   The guards stepped out first, and Lord Gizak followed, a strange picture of opulence.   His resemblance to the Baroness was both uncanny and unsettling, and he was dressed in clothes of a richness rarely seen, while his men were very well equipped in shining armor without even a hint of a dent.   She wondered if Gizak's embroidered tunic was something found in these marvelous ruins, costuming from a time long past.   He wore a gold sash across his chest, glittering with baubles and gems, and his hair was slicked back with a pomade that also had been used on his thin, stylized moustache.   A short cape of flowing blue velvet fell from his shoulders, and he walked with the gait of someone with a much more regal standing than some provincial village lord.   The Slayer felt many of her companions shift beside her, as though embarrassed by their own shabby appearance. She found herself standing straighter, wishing she'd been even more covered with scrapes and cuts and gore to counteract his polished appearance.

A young man stalked behind him, shoulders hunched as though trying to disappear into himself, into the brocade tunic covering his adolescent body. The resemblance to Lord Gizak placed him easily as an elder son. The younger children, so well behaved up to that point, leapt to their feet and rushed toward their father, throwing their arms around his legs with delighted cries, despite the disdainful looks they earned from their mother. As they clung, Lord Gizak laughed, a hearty and warm sound that abruptly differentiated him from his cold and calculating sister.

"What terrible guards!" he laughed, rifling his hands through the children's hair. "Attacked by Soulless, and they don't even lift a finger to protect me!"

One of the children, squealing in delight, proceeded to pretend to gnaw on his leg, while the other begged between giggles, "No, no, it's me, Father, it's me! I'm not a Soulless!"

"Honestly, children! Gizak!" His wife had one hand to her chest and the other rested on her forehead, where a predictably constant headache was probably growing stronger. "Can we at least pretend to be a little dignified? You have guests."

She did not gesture toward the group so much as she merely jerked her head their way, wide-eyed and warning. The Slayer nearly missed it, having closed her eyes at the children's strange playfulness. It was clearly just a game to them, but she found the thought of anyone pretending to be a monster abhorrent, and it made that heated temper of hers surge through her blood. Lord Gizak blinked at his wife for a moment before following her gesture and duly taking in the sight of them, the chuckle dying in his throat.

"Ah, yes," he said, shaking the children off. They sulked and groaned at the dismissal, but they seemed to understand the concept of business and shuffled morosely back to their seats. The older boy also sat, but Lord Gizak went to bow before the Slayer and her retinue. "They told me you had arrived. Did they forget to offer you accommodations? You look rather rough from the road, if I may say so."

"You may," the Slayer said, unsure of how to answer. "We do not wish to stay, my lord, we only wish to deliver some news to you. We come to you from Para—"

"And who might this be?" the Lord asked, cutting the Slayer off and moving toward Veroh, his brow creased in thought. His fingers twisted the ends of his moustache as Veroh stiffened. She kept still, though, which was more than what the Slayer would have been able to manage with his leering eyes. Behind him, Lady Gizak's gaze hardened, boring into her husband's back. "I know I've seen this face before."

Veroh cleared her throat, but could not clear the bright red sneaking up into her cheeks. "Yes, about a year ago, I'd guess," she said. "You have an excellent memory, my lord. I am..er, was...a part of your sister's court."

Lord Gizak said, snapping his fingers and beaming with delight, though his realization seemed to make Veroh all the more uncomfortable. "Yes, of course, that's where I've seen you before! Oh, please don't tell me she's sent you, I've already informed her that our potato crop is suffering as it is, but we might be able to make an exception if only she'd--"

"Gizak." His wife interrupted him with a voice that was deceptively soft. "The girl said she was a part of her court."

He seemed confused by Lady Gizak's gentle insertion, but, again, realization came to him quickly. "Was? Has something happened? I can't imagine her casting out a servant such as yourself. If I recall correctly, you were one of her most accommodating and clever little—"

"We come to tell you that Paravelle is no more." The Captain of the Guard cut in harshly, his voice a sharp rapport unlike anything the Slayer had heard from him before. It had the firmness of how he spoke to his soldiers, though there was a simmering anger there, burning in his dark eyes as he stared firmly into Lord Gizak. She realized that a tension seemed to stretch between the three of them, Lord Gizak, the Captain, and Veroh, though she couldn't quite understand it. Veroh dropped her eyes, and the Captain had his fist balled up tightly.

"It has become overrun with Soulless," he explained further, each word forced and firm. "Your sister is dead, as well as nearly everyone inside by now. We and a few others are all that escaped that night. Veroh thought you should know."

All flippancy was gone from the man, leaving only bewilderment. His eyes danced between Veroh and the Captain, occasionally settling on the Slayer. Several times, he seemed ready to speak, but then the cloud of confusion darkened his face even more, and he reconsidered. "How is that even possible?" he asked.

Both Veroh and the Captain drew in a breath of hesitation. The Slayer knew there was something going on, unspoken, between the two of them, though she couldn't fathom what it was. It kept her from providing her own explanation, knowing she would likely ruin whatever fine nuances they were trying to establish.

She hadn't felt so lost and out of place since she was a child, struggling to find her father's sword in the ashes of their homestead.

"We don't know," Veroh managed. "But we hope to find out, which is why we must move on to find the Queen. I'm terribly sorry for your loss, my lord. It must be difficult to hear."

Lord Gizak sunk into his throne, burying his head in his hands for a moment. Why wasn't Veroh telling him the truth? The Slayer had to clench her fists together to keep from pouring out her fury.

"My loss?" Lord Gizak looked up at them with an astonished face, gone pale and stark. "What about yours? Your homes, your family, all gone, just like that, and no one could have seen it coming. If Paravelle isn't safe, then...no one is."

The implication hung in the air, heavy and palpable. "It might be wise to increase your defences even more, my lord," the Captain suggested. "There are truly strange times ahead of us."

"Yes," Lord Gizak murmured. "Yes, indeed. Thank you. Thank you for telling me. Take whatever you need with you, I'll have my guards supply you with whatever you may desire to help your journey. Horses, weapons, anything, if it helps you get the word to the Queen faster. I'm not sure what she might do to help, if anything, but she should at least know."

"Shouldn't he know?" the Slayer whispered to Veroh, once they had thanked Lord Gizak for his offer, but explained that they just wanted to be on their way after they replenished their food supply. She glanced over her shoulder to where Lady Gizak had gone to comfort her husband, as had the two young children, though they didn't seem to comprehend what had upset their father so. Lady Gizak must have noticed her looking, because the woman lifted her eyes and they lingered on the departing group. "I think the wife knows that we're keeping something from him."

"What good would it do?" Veroh whispered back. "Let him grieve for his sister without the knowledge of the monster she became."

"And if he was in on it?" Kyle hissed, butting his way into the conversation. "This is her brother! Don't you think it's strange how peaceful it is here, too? Didn't you say that the Soulless were listening to what the Baroness told them?"

"Now is not the time or place for such discussions," the Captain said, giving them all a warning glance as his eyes took in the soldiers surrounding them. "For now, let us be rid of this place and get back to the mission at hand. Maybe the Queen can help us understand just how broadly this reaches."

The disturbing thought that maybe, just maybe, Lord Gizak had been involved in his sister's sick machinations twisted the Slayer's gut, but one look back at the man's despair convinced her otherwise. What she couldn't so easily discern, however, was the strange, haunted, somewhat accusing eyes of his wife, following them as they departed.

CHAPTER THIRTEEN

As they started back on the rambling road heading toward the City on the Lake, the journey seemed to weigh heavily on everyone's weary shoulders. It seemed as though they could traverse the whole world, from the impenetrable forests all the way to the endless sea, and never gain even a glimpse of the Queen's airship in the big blue sky. After leaving Lord Gizak's village, spirits were low and resolve seemed even lower.

"We're never going to find her," Kyle grumbled. "She's probably all the way on the other side of the world. Even better, I bet we missed her. She probably passed over us while we were wasting time with that Lord Gizak."

"Surely, we can't be that much further from the City on the Lake," Veroh reasoned. "We just have to keep moving. Though, truly, if we do not find sign of the Queen by then, perhaps the City will be a good place to settle and rethink our plans. We'll come by her eventually, I'm sure, but I'm not so sure we're all cut out for this constant roaming."

"Should we take to the woods?" one of them, the girl from the second village, asked. "The trees would provide some cover, especially if those ominous clouds mean more rain on our heads."

"Then how will we see the Queen if she's nearby?" the Slayer asked. "They will provide good cover for when we need to rest, though, so we shall skirt the outside. Keep your eyes to the sky and your ears to the woods. Who knows how many Soulless are benefiting from the cover of leaves and shadow in there as well?"

Evening descended without further incident, the clouds still threatening, and it did not take long for them to find a comfortable spot in the woods still deep enough for cover. They would keep two watches at a time, one for the ground and one to climb into the canopy and watch for the Queen's airship. Missing it in the night would be a tragedy that none of them wanted.

Whoever did the ground watch while the Slayer took her rest, though, was not doing a very good job. Kyle, no doubt. Through her customary light sleep, she heard a twig snap. Her eyes flew open, but she didn't move a muscle, not yet. She listened and waited, to better assess the threat. More than likely, it was just an animal, especially since the woods were still and silent after the snap. A Soulless would have kept ambling, rustling leaves as it went, and, eventually, it would moan, like gas escaping a corpse. None of those sounds followed, but she did start to discern breathing, quick and nervous, not the steady slow slumbering breaths of her companions.

The breathing was followed by slow footsteps, carefully made but easily noticed with ears such as her own. They were very close to her, and they were getting closer. She could practically feel the body looming over her, but she waited until the very last second to act. She moved like a viper, reaching for her dagger and turning just in time to snatch the arm of the person approaching with her other hand. She pulled the body in, rolling, twisting the person's arm as she threw it down and climbed on top of it. Her blade went smoothly under the neck, pressing upwards while she pulled the person's head up by his hair.

"Who are you?" she whispered, careful not to wake the others. Not yet. Not unless it was absolutely necessary. "What are you doing here?"

A loud, rasping voice started to answer, but she pushed the blade against his flesh. He whimpered slightly, squirming underneath her, and she noted how compact and thin his body was. "Quietly," she said. "No need to disturb the others if we don't have to. Now, tell me, quietly, who you are and what you are doing here."

Her captive squirmed again, just enough to have the blade graze his skin, and he abruptly stopped. "I-I am sorry," he whispered back, though he sounded like he wanted to howl the words in panic. "Please. I meant no harm. I was only following--"

"That much is clear. Who are you? Why are you following us? Answer these questions, and you will not be forced to bear a new necklace of your own blood."

"P-Please!" he stammered. "Please! I..I am Renald de Gizak, Lord Gizak's son! Please don't hurt me! I only wanted to come with you, to...to find the Queen. Please, I meant no harm."

"Lord Gizak's son?" she asked, lightening the pressure from her blade and, when he didn't immediately try to scamper off, she let him go completely. In the darkness, she slowly began to realize that he was must have been the older boy in the throne room, the quiet one who had been playing chess with his father before they arrived.

"How long have you been following us?" she asked, a feeling of surprise and shock creeping over her as they both stood; she had to offer a sturdy arm to help him to his feet. "Since we left your father's company?"

"Aye," he said, the slightest hint of a proud grin on his face, "that's right. I waited to be dismissed and then hurriedly grabbed my things. It had been a while since we've had adventurers come through, and I vowed one day to sneak away with them. Your party was even better than I could have hoped, for while I truly want to be away from my father's house, my ultimate goal is to meet the Queen. She rarely stops by our village, and when she does, it is for a brief time and she never leaves her ship."

The Slayer did not reply at first, listening as whoever was on guard finally heard their scuffle and was edging over to investigate. She could see the dark form slowly creeping toward them. "It's all right," she called, no longer concerned with keeping so quiet. "It's me. And an unexpected guest."

Veroh stepped forward, her eyes wide in shocked wonder. "I am so sorry!" she said, hands to her chest as though her heart couldn't handle imagining all the things that could have happened due to her faulty watch. "I swear, I heard nothing. It was so quiet and still, I couldn't have imagined someone could be out here."

"Don't worry," the Slayer assured her. "He is very good at being undetected, and he means us no harm. You're not going to believe this, though. It's none other than Lord Gizak's eldest son."

"Lord Gizak's?" A dark shadow of confusion passed over Veroh's face. "Whatever for?"

"Please." Renald turned his plea to Veroh, clutching his hands together like some beggar in a story play. "I want to go with you. I needed to get out of that place; I can't stand it anymore. I know it's safe, but I also know there is so much more to the world than hiding in dusty relics of the past. I want to come with you. I want to see the Queen."

"He's lying." The others were waking, and it did not take long for the suspicious Kyle to join this discussion. "Join us? What nonsense! Why not just ask before we left? We've taken in riff raff from across the world, why would he be an exception? He's spying on us, that's what it is. You saw the look on his mother's face, boring into us, accusing us, accusing Veroh."

"I don't think I like what you're implying there, soldier," the Captain put in grimly, fixing Kyle with a hard stare before his eyes drifted around the group, to Veroh suddenly stiff and quiet, to the Slayer, to the bug-eyed Renald. "What's going on here?"

The Slayer was about to explain before Renald jumped in for himself. "I left my father's court," he said, "because I had to get out of there. I couldn't stand it anymore; it was like a prison! Then you all showed up, and you were looking for the Queen, and...I've heard that the Queen holds in her court a scholar of ancient texts from before the epidemic. I have so many questions, and Father has no answers. Surely, the Queen's court will! Please, let me come with you. I'm not much of a fighter, I'll admit that, but I can hold my own, and I won't be a bother or a nuisance."

"But you could be a spy," Kyle accused, "or a plant or some other danger. How can you honestly expect us to trust you if you've been following us like someone who can't be trusted?"

"I couldn't have just asked!" Renald burst not with embarrassment but with fury. "Father would never allow it. He doesn't believe in the outside world, and thinks the only place for us is there inside those old walls. And I didn't want you to send me back, so I waited."

"And snuck up on me in the middle of the night?" the Slayer ventured, folding her arms in front of her.

Renald bit his lip, his hands drifting down to his stomach. "I was hungry," he said sheepishly. "I've never really left the kingdom before and didn't think of food. I thought maybe I could sneak some from your pack without you noticing, but, clearly, I was wrong."

"Clearly," the Slayer grunted. "Have you ever actually seen a Soulless attack, Renald?"

Slowly, sadly, he shook his head, eyes wide in the flickering light of their torches. "No," he said, "not first-hand. I'd read accounts, of course, and planned strategies for such battles, but, as I said, Father barely lets us leave the manor when things are fine. Just imagine how he tries to keep us in when there's actually a threat. It's been a while since we've had an attack that close to the village, anyway. The guards do well to keep us safe."

"And if you did encounter a Soulless, right here, right now?" the Slayer asked. "How do you think you would handle it?"

With the color drained from his face, Renald seemed to glow in the torchlight, his eyes seeming too big, the apple in his throat bobbing significantly as he tried to swallow his fear. "As best I could, ma'am," he managed. "You have to go for the head, don't you? I have a dagger. I would focus on using it to get through their skulls to their brains, by whatever means necessary."

"Are you sure?" the Slayer pressed. "It's not too far for you to turn back now. We've already lost others and they were trained soldiers who had fought Soulless before. It won't all be some grand adventure like in your storybooks."

"I know," Renald said, his resolve strengthening. "I know. But I can't go back there, not now that I'm finally away. I need to see the world. I want to see the Soulless. I want to see the Queen and talk with her scholars about all the things my father holds so dear about the ancient world. Please. I want to be here."

"That's all I need," she said, backed by a chorus of agreeing grunts from the others. "Don't worry; we'll get you to the Queen. Perhaps our different goals will intersect, and we'll be helping each other. Now, since we're all up already, let's pack it up, we may as well get an early start. Renald, why don't you help the Captain of the Guard and see what he might be able to spare by way of armor for you."

She was pleased to see everyone, especially their new addition, spurn immediately into action. Her small army continued to grow, though she had to remind herself that it would matter much if they didn't figure out what to do soon. At this rate, Veroh was right. If they didn't find the Queen by the time they reached the City on the Lake, they might as well leave Paravelle as a bad memory and get on with things as they were, especially if the plague of Paravelle remained locked within its sturdy walls.

CHAPTER FOURTEEN

A few days later, they took a small respite by a stream, the weather warm and pleasant, the location a good spot to rest and renew. They had come across one village kind enough to give them a little food, but too nervous to let them linger, and then an abandoned settlement with a few Soulless roaming about. They were quickly dispatched, giving Renald a light taste of what he was in store for when they came across a much larger and brutal swarm later that evening. His shock was immense, but he recovered quickly, shoving his fear aside to join the fight for his life.

Not only had Renald had adapted to the Soulless easily, he adapted to the group rather well, too, proving himself to be bright and eager. When the others were preparing a meal for the night, he would slip away with the Captain and Kyle to learn how to properly fight. He had the showy style of a trained fencer, but he quickly learned that Soulless required a more brutal approach. He tired easily, unaccustomed to such physical work, but even as they rested, he bubbled with questions about techniques and battles. The Captain was eager to answer, too; it was clear that he missed leading new troops into the exciting territories of soldiership.

"It's nice," Veroh sighed wistfully once a stew was finished and distributed among their small group. She settled beside the Slayer, where she sat atop an outcropping of rocks, watching the group as well as the horizon. All was calm and serene and quiet, without even a hint of a bad feeling. "To be able to sit here and just be for a while. That was something I think I started to take for granted back in Paravelle, but it does make you wonder. What if the world could actually be like this?"

"It might have been," Renald said with an eager sort of smile, cheeks glowing pink, which brought out his freckles. "Once upon a time. I've seen pictures and maps in some of those old books. That's why I want to learn more about them. It could show a whole new world, an old world, a world before the Soulless. Maybe we can get back to it someday."

"That's mighty idealistic," Kyle grunted. "How can there be a world without Soulless? They're everywhere, and there will always be more. For every one that we kill, there's another making five more. Not to mention if there are probably others like the Baroness, harboring them like a psychopath."

"What do you mean?" Renald asked, confusion casting the eagerness out of his face. A hush fell over them as the realization hit them like a brick that he didn't know the true reason for their quest. The Slayer shot a cold look toward Veroh and the Captain, who had so delicately danced away from it with Lord Gizak, and she decided to take the task up herself.

"We should be honest with you about something," she said. "It was deemed unnecessary to tell your father, but, since you are travelling with us, you should know something else about the attack on Paravelle. The Baroness was behind it all. Not only was she keeping bodies that the people though were destroyed in a giant pit below the fortress, to turn them into Soulless, but she released them on the people during the night, and she somehow was able to control them. Order them. Tell them what to do, like an army. That, more than anything, is why we seek the Queen. She should know how the Baroness has betrayed her kingdom."

For all the bright sunshine and the babbling brook, a darkness seemed to have passed over them as Renald, his jaw hanging slack, tried to take this information in. "No," he finally managed, quietly. "No, that can't be. Why would she do such a thing?"

"We were wondering that same thing ourselves," Veroh said, moving over to sit beside him and putting an arm around his slim shoulders. "We think that, maybe, she had done it because the Slayer was there, hoping to kill her in the night, and to cover the murder with the tragedy. She was pretending to try to save some of us, but she dropped all pretense once she realized that the Slayer hadn't been killed at all."

"Kill the Slayer of the Soulless!" Renald remarked. "That's absurd. Why would anyone want to do something like that?"

"Attempting to understand the Baroness is futile," the Slayer said. "She's dead now, and, whatever her reasons, she was able to control those Soulless. We hope to get to the bottom of this, but, more than likely, we won't. Still, though, you should know."

The peacefulness of the scene had died entirely, as it lapsed into a reflective silence, Renald struggling to put the pieces of their story together. He took it all quietly, and the Slayer felt a little admiration for his ability to be so objective. It was clearly difficult for him to grasp the idea, but he didn't rail against them, he didn't bemoan the tragedy, he didn't get too upset. He took it in and considered it objectively, as one might when their opponent made an unexpected move that forced them to reconsider their strategy in chess.

The next day, they were attacked at another settlement, where they helped them control the latest swarm coming in from the north, where they must have demolished a group. They move with swiftness and strength, a clear sign that they had been feeding, but they did not have the same luck in this riverside village. It was there that they also learned that they were getting very close to the City on the Lake. All they had to do was follow the river, which fed into the large body of water that protected the city as effectively as Paravelle's stone walls once protected it. For whatever reason, the Soulless were incapable of crossing a body of water deeper than their knees, so, filling their boats, the people of the City on the Lake sailed off to an in island in the middle of the largest lake they could find, and there they settled. Smaller than Paravelle and without as much prosperity, the island appealed to many, but they developed a program with migration. A ring of Soulless always seemed to surround the place, waiting for anyone coming or going, making it difficult and dangerous for anyone wishing to cross.

Questions of the Queen received positive, hopeful responses, as well. It seemed that the rumors that she would be heading to the City on the Lake were likely close to truth, convincing them to stay the path, and hopefully, they would not need to stay for long before the supposed event occurred. Of course, if the Queen was on her way, there was a good chance it was because of increased activity in the area, so they prepared themselves to cleave a bloody path to the lake.

Her suspicions were entirely correct. It seemed as though they couldn't move two feet without encountering a Soulless, but the strange thing was how they were spread out, in tiny clusters, two or three of them milling around together, or perhaps five or six. Of course, once they got the attention of one, the small group nearby would notice and come to explore, and several of Soulless on the other side of the river tried splashing through to reach them, but only made it so far. They moaned and groaned as they tried to reach across the current; they had arrows to quiet them, as their sounds would attract more Soulless, but they didn't want to waste their arrows, especially not when the Soulless were steadily coming regardless.

As they neared the City on the Lake, knowing it to be just over the ridge of hills ahead, the Slayer felt a bad twist in her stomach, a sudden clench of dread. They had cleared themselves of Soulless on their side of the river, though they knew more to await for them beyond the next hill, but nothing could prepare them for what truly awaited them when they cautiously climbed it and looked down on the wide valley that spread out before the lake.

Like debris brought in by the ocean's powerful tides, a thick ring of Soulless surrounded the large lake. Fifteen deep at some spots, their decaying bodies nudged and bumped each other in a half-hearted attempt to get to the water's edge. Once there, they stopped, unable to continue. With each minute that passed a few more Soulless trickled over the surrounding hills and into the valley, as if called by some summons normal ears could not hear. Even the dock that held the ferry to take people over was overrun with them, several of them rolling limply in the water after having been shoved off the dock by the nudging shoulders of the others.

No one dared to say a word. The moans from the Soulless surrounding the City were so loud that the sounds of the ones across the river would be lost, but surely they would still be attracted by anything much louder. Thank the stars no one screamed. If just one of those Soulless noticed them, the others would realize that there was fresh flesh over that hill, and every one of them would descend upon them. The Slayer made a gesture, as small as she could manage, and slowly backed away from the crest of the hill.

"So much for that idea," Kyle murmured, voice barely above a whisper. "The only way to get into that place now is to be air lifted and dropped off by the Queen herself."

"Why are they doing that?" Renald asked. "There's so many of them. Don't they know they can't get through?"

"They can sense that there are people on the other side of that water," the Slayer said, though it was mostly a guess. "I've seen it before, but never like this. They don't have the capacity to reason as we do. All they can do is sense things and follow the most basic carnal impulses. The last time I was in this area, years ago, there was only a small group, which were easily taken care of. You had to be quick and fight your way to the ferry, but you could get there."

"So what do we do now?" the Captain asked. "I think it's clear that we won't be sailing over to the City on the Lake any time soon."

"I suppose we turn around," the Slayer said, "and head back the way toward the last village. Sometimes, the Queen will stop along the fringe settlements as well, providing supplies and—"

As they turned, though, she stopped suddenly, staring off into the sky as she thought she saw something. She wasn't the only one. "What is that?" Veroh asked, narrowing her eyes against the right sunlight. "That black dot on the horizon?"

"Unbelievable!" the Slayer gasped, once her eyes adjusted to the burning brightness. "The Queen's airship!"

"And not a moment too soon," Kyle groaned, his own attention pointing their gaze off to the side. "Look!"

Coming in from the side was a new swarm of Soulless, ambling toward them with dedication. The Slayer felt a hiss of a curse push past her teeth, as she wildly tried to determine the distance of the airship from where they were. Too far, that was all she knew, but she was drawing her steel, preparing for the battle though her mind reeled on trying to figure out how not to lose the Queen's ship.

"Quickly!" she ordered. "Let's get as far from the hill as we possibly can before they reach us. We don't need any of that mess around the city to come spilling over toward us. Then someone, while we fend off the Soulless, make a fire, big as you can, so that the navigators will hopefully notice the smoke and give us a second glance. Hurry! Before more of them come!"

The Slayer glanced upwards, trying to relocate the approaching black dot. Still far away, still heading toward them. If it was moving slowly enough, they would have enough time, but if it was moving too slowly, it might be too late. When she hacked through the approaching Soulless, she threw the bodies into the small fire that the foothill soldiers had started, causing the flames to leap up and the smoke to darken. It would make an excellent signal, and they could keep feeding it, but it seemed that, the more they killed, the more arrived, tempted by all the sounds and the smell of blood and fire.

As they fought, as the battle became more brutal, the ship was getting closer and closer and ready to pass them by. Furious and frustrated, the Slayer fought with everything she had, each blow more powerful than the last. But she was starting to feel overwhelmed. She heard a scream of pain from someone, shouts from someone else as a Soulless ripped into him. Where had they all come from? Could the Soulless from the lake have gotten to them so quickly? Time could be funny like that; what seemed like the blink of an eye in battle turned out to be several long minutes. What started as a trickle grew into a flood, and the hideous creatures were sweeping them away.

Which of her comrades had fallen prey to the ravenous horde? Though her heart, heavy with dread, seemed to settle in her stomach, she couldn't worry about it now. She had to focus on herself first; that was the first rule of survival. As she fought, though, she began to fear that more deaths would follow. She was blind to the action around her, seeing only the Soulless in front of her, their black blood splattering all over her and the force of her sword. The crackling of the fire seemed to roar, and she couldn't tell if the screams she was hearing were those of her companions or merely the screaming in her own head. There were so many of them, and they seemed so incredibly strong. Where had they all come from? How had they become so overwhelmed so quickly?

Her limbs became heavy with hopelessness, and her head was pounding in a way she couldn't understand. Her actions were mechanical, her sword swinging and smashing as though disembodied from her mind, which seemed dull and suddenly unable to concentrate. Her breath came out in rasping, struggling breaths. A dark shadow seemed to pass over them, perhaps the airship, perhaps the final grip of death. Had she been bitten and, in the chaos, didn't realize it? She didn't have time to find out. She had to keep fighting, she had to keep going. She heard shouting, but ignored it, slashing through another body. More shouting, closer now, and a distinct curse. Finally, a voice boomed, breaking through the dark haze that had taken over her.

"Look up!"

Blinking, feeling numb, the Slayer did just that, right in time to see a man dangling from the sky and holding out his hand. "Quick!" he shouted. "Grab on!"

At first, she could only stare in confusion, but she managed to look past the man to the massive looming hull of the Queen's ship. The man clung to a rope later with his other hand, and she followed the line of the ladder to the open hatch in the belly of the ship. She reached for the offered hand. They must have seen the battle from above and swooped down to save them, and now they were being pulled up and away from the horde to safety. She wondered how much longer they could have held out; she was sure she could fight her way through all those Soulless, but she couldn't say the same for the rest of her party.

Once inside the safety of the hull, the Slayer needed a moment to recover, her brain still heavily on the carnage that had occurred down below. She felt as though her field of vision was still tinged by the blackness of her bloodlust, her limbs were still aching to be swinging her sword and attacking. It happened often, in the middle of a battle, where something deep within her took over, and it was all about the fighting until there was nothing left to fight. Pulled from the zone in the middle of it was a jarring experience, and it took her a while to come back, slumped against the wall and catching her breath.

"Who's here?" she finally demanded, blinking to let her eyes adjust to the darkness of the ship's hull. Faint lights along the wall glowed slightly, unnatural and strange. "Who's missing?"

At first, she thought with a shock that Renald hadn't made it, but then she saw the young lord's coppery hair as he was being lifted through another hatch. The Captain of the Guard clung to a shaken Veroh, and Kyle was slumped against the opposite wall, his head tilted back, face pale as he choked down sobs. That was it. There was no sign of the others, those eager soldiers and the brave girl that had joined them. Something twisted hard in the Slayer's gut, as she told herself to just wait a moment, and they would appear.

But they didn't. Veroh's eyes caught hers at the moment of realization, and a slow, pained groan escaped the young woman, closing her eyes tightly as she leaned into the Captain's chest.

"You're lucky we got there when we did," one of the Queen's soldiers said, offering the Slayer a canteen of water and a damp cloth to wipe the visceral of battle from her face. "What a swarm! We could see them converging from all the way up here, and then we realized they were converging on people!"

"Thank you," the Slayer said, taking the canteen and leaving the cloth hanging in the soldier's hands as she drank from it, deep and slow, letting the cool water calm her nerves and settle her racing heart. When she finished, the canteen was empty, and it fell from her loose fingers with a thump as she nearly slid down the wall to the floor. "I'm just glad we finally found you. We've been searching for days."

"Weeks!" Kyle corrected with a groan. "Though the days do blend together after a while."

"So this is it," Veroh murmured, looking around with sadness and exhaustion still in her eyes. She seemed to wince, and the Slayer wondered what was going on in her head, if her brain was replaying the battle below and she was trying to push it away. "The Queen's airship. We finally made it."

"We have to see her," the Slayer said, grappling onto the task at hand to help her focus. She pushed herself back up the wall, steading herself on her feet, and fixing the soldier with a steady, unwavering gaze. "Take us to the Queen at once. We have grave and dire news to deliver to her, and the sooner, the better."

The soldier lifted one cool brow, looked the Slayer up and down, and said, "Not like that, you aren't. Some of you have obtained wounds and must be treated, and we have to ensure none have been bitten. The last thing we'd want is an outbreak aboard the ship."

"What happens if one of us are bitten?" Kyle asked, holding his shoulder, which was scraped of its cloth and red with gore. As soon as he spoke, he seemed to realize what it looked like and his eyes went wide. "I mean, I haven't been, obviously. This is just a scratch. But what if someone was? You'd have to kill them, won't you?"

"If they'd been bitten," the soldier said darkly, "they're practically dead already. We do what we must to keep it from spreading."

Though it didn't seem possible, Kyle's face grew even paler as he swallowed down something caught in his throat. His hand didn't move from his shoulder, despite a soldier's attempt to clean it off with another damp cloth.

The Slayer had to admit that she was reluctant to receive treatment, as well, feeling her heart racing at the idea of being poked and prodded by the Queen's medical staff. She had been in that position once before, not too long ago, and it send a shiver dancing up her spine. But as she pushed from the wall, she realized she walked with a limp, and it was easy to tell that the others were worse for wear, physically as well as emotionally. She also knew the soldiers would refuse to take her to the Queen until they had been checked out. She could find them, she knew that for sure, could somehow find the energy to hack her way there, but it had already been weeks since they left Paravelle. What was another day? She just hoped they would be quick with their business, and then they could get back to theirs.

CHAPTER FIFTEEN

Waking with a start, the Slayer had forgotten entirely where she was, confused by the cold white walls that surrounded her and the soft cushioned mattress underneath her. The air was filled with the steady, thumping hum of the airship's engines, making her feel as though she were in the belly of some living thing rather than a mechanical wonder. Slowly, she began to place herself, deducing from her immaculate surroundings and the bandages on her wounds that she was in the medical ward of the Queen's airship. It irritated her that her clothes and armor had been removed to be replaced by a sterile white shift, but at least they were at arm's reach on a nearby chair, along with her sword and dagger and her heavy, skull-crushing boots.

It was a small room, with four beds, though only one other was occupied, by an older woman she did not know. One bed looked as though it had been previously occupied, and the Slayer figured that bed must have been Veroh's. The young woman was on her feet, dressed in the same white shift as the Slayer, pacing the room back and forth. A deep red scar burned on her cheek, and a bandage peeked out from under the short sleeve of her shift. She halted when she heard the Slayer sitting up in her bed, dark curls shaken loose from the ribbon that tried to hold her hair back.

"They said you might not be up for another hour or so," she remarked, clearly surprised but a little pleased. Her face was pale with worry, her hands hanging as though she'd been wringing them far too much.

"Perhaps," she said, grimacing slightly, "if I were anyone else that might be true. Sleep is generally something I avoid if I can help it. It's a luxury I can't afford."

"Not even now?" Veroh asked. "We're on the ship. We're safe. You should take advantage of that."

"I don't think I could even if I wanted to." The Slayer pulled back the thin white sheet, throwing her legs over the side to find the floor with her bare toes. Wiggling them, she couldn't help noticing how calloused and dry they were, how her left foot was forever slightly distorted from a time when Soulless tried to bite off her foot even through her heavy metal boots. Thinking of it made her bite her lip, wondering what might have happened if it had gotten through, if she would be staring at a mechanical leg like Thom's just then. "We've already wasted more time than I'd like with resting. We should find the Queen, and soon."

She didn't need to say another word; she only had to nod slightly, and Veroh was there to help her change back into her armor. "I assume the men have been separated into their own room," the Slayer said, glancing over her shoulder as Veroh buckled the leather straps of her breastplate, cinching her into the familiar metal vest. Encased in steel once more, she started to less vulnerable and more like herself again.

"Yes," Veroh said, "I think so. I haven't gone to see, but I'm sure they're fine. Thank the stars they showed up when they did, or else I don't think most of us would have made it."

"Mm." Perhaps it was just the effect these cold white rooms had on her, but the Slayer felt a slight bit of suspicion suddenly. The ship had arrived in a timely fashion; was there more to it than mere coincidence? She had to shake those thoughts out of her head, though, deciding that Paravelle had made her feel a little paranoid and cautious.

"Let's go," she said, boots and grieves firmly in place, but she didn't get very far. As she and Veroh headed for the door, a woman came through it, dressed in slightly stained white robes. She seemed startled to see the two of the up and about, but she recovered quickly. "You're awake," she remarked, laughing a little to take the edge off her surprise. "You must have slept well to have recovered so quickly."

"We don't have time to waste on sleeping," the Slayer said. "We wish to find our other companions, and then to see the Queen. Can you take us to her?"

The woman struggled with an answer, gaping like a fish. "Well, I don't think...I mean, I've only just come to make sure everything was all right."

"If you can't take us to the Queen," the Slayer said, carefully measuring her voice with forced patience, "will you take us to someone who can? Point us in the right direction?"

The woman still faltered, the hopelessness and confusion growing on her face. "Fine, then," the Slayer cut in, pushing by her, "we'll manage on our own. Come on, Veroh."

"Wait!" They had only made it a few steps before the woman found her voice at last. "Hold on. You should really stay in your room, the both of you, but I can see that you won't. At least go see the Doctor first. He'll want to follow up with you, and then he can take you to the Queen."

The Slayer stopped abruptly, as if that title had struck her and rendered her motionless. Of course, deep inside her logical brain, she knew he had to be around here somewhere, but she had not confronted the fact outright. The mere thought of him sent her blood thumping in her veins, matched to the gentle thumping of the airship itself, pounding in her head. She curled her fist at her side, feeling it damp with sweat. He was the last person she would want to see right then.

"Please," the woman said, "it'll take but a minute. He'd boot me straight back to the kitchens for good if he knew I let you go see the Queen without talking to him first."

Jaw clenched tight, the Slayer weighed her options, considering how ineffective it would be to just blaze through and find the Queen herself. She knew the ship to be deceptively large, difficult to navigate as its insides were a mess of hallways and rooms, tangled and twisting. She closed her eyes, trying to calm her racing heart.

"Fine," she murmured, without opening her eyes yet. "But only if it's quick."

"Of course," the woman's head bobbed. "It will. We know your time is valuable, Slayer."

She brushed past them, her steps quick down the narrow hallway, pitching slightly as the world shifted, the airship caught on a strong air current. The Slayer reached out to steady herself against a wall, stepping forward carefully. When the ship listed, it felt as though one was suddenly inebriated, the floor surging like a wave under her feet. Veroh had difficulty, too, but, eventually, it evened out, and they had made a few turns to lead them to a door with a small brass plaque on it.

The woman gave it a few smart knocks. "Doctor," she called, "it's Alice. I have the patients from room two with me. We're coming in."

Beyond the door, which creaked slightly on its hinges, was a square room with several desks and table and chairs bolted down to the floor. A small man with very little hair on his shining head looked over from where he was putting a book back on a shelf. His shoulders were slightly stooped, and his face looked much older when considered for a second time. He peered at them through round little glasses, narrowing his dark, beady eyes. "Ah, yes," he said, turning to face them completely. "The Slayer returns and still refuses proper medical treatment, I see. Some things never change."

"We need to see the Queen" the Slayer said, "but this woman suggested we see you first. You can take us to her, can't you? I don't like wasting time."

"Oh, I'm sure you don't." Face wrinkling, there was a sparkle of amusement in the man's eyes. "Always with your head on the ground, forgetting that time flows differently here. Down there, it's always quick, quick, quick, get a move on, on to the next Soulless. Up here, there are only the clouds and the birds and the gentle hum of the engines. We'll reach our destination when we get there, no point in rushing it along."

She narrowed her eyes at him, bristling as this pretentious speech. "I am not a creature of the air," she said. "The sooner I get my feet back on the ground, the better."

The Doctor tilted his head, looking at her thoughtfully, his smile bemused and contrite. "And what of the others in your party?" he asked. "We'd best get you all together at once, so we don't unnecessarily bother the Queen with multiple visitations. Alice, be a dear, won't you? Why don't you take the Slayer's companion to go and fetch the others in their party, and we'll all head to the Queen together?"

Alice didn't hesitate, but Veroh did. The Slayer didn't break her untrustworthy gaze with the Doctor, but she gave Veroh a subtle nod. "It's fine, Veroh," she said, flexing and curling her fists at her side, though not in anticipation of grabbing her weapons for a change. It was just the memory of what had happened the last time she had been in this office, in the presence of this man. And it was a demon she would rather face without Veroh there.

For a moment, the Slayer thought Veroh was going to refuse, but she ultimately nodded and agreed. Awkward silence prevailed until they had gone, the door closed tightly behind them. The ship tilted a little to one side, but she stood steady and strong, as did he.

"Didn't think I'd see you back for a while," the Doctor finally spoke, his voice somewhat soft and distant. A faint smile turned the corner of his mouth.

"I was hoping I could do this without seeing you," she said. "I suppose I shouldn't be surprised you would sweep in and collect us right through the gate."

"You were under Soulless attack," the Doctor said simply. "What were we to do? March you straight to the Queen without examining you? I think not. You're looking well, though. How are you feeling?"

"Fine," the Slayer managed, though it took some work to loosen her jaw. She became suddenly aware of everything her body was doing, the pounding of her heart, the sweat on her palms, the blood running through her veins. And it was then that she remembered the small vial she had found on the Baroness, and the fact that it was no longer in her pouch. How in the world could she have forgotten it? Suddenly, its unexpected absence seemed to slap her in the face. "I feel fine."

"Good, good!" The Doctor was clearly delighted, perhaps too much so, his joviality hiding something else. "That's excellent to hear. So everything has been fine since our last visit? No odd feelings or compulsions or relapses?"

"No," she said tightly, trying to push back all the instances she could remember where she started to feel sick or irrationally angry or oddly overcome with weakness, much as she had earlier in the swarm before they had been lifted up by the Queen's soldiers. They were rare, but she knew if she mentioned them, the Doctor would turn those molehills into mountains and attempt to get her to succumb to his work once again.

"Wonderful!" the Doctor beamed outright now, making a few scribbles on a piece of paper. "Before we part ways, you must allow me to follow up with a check-in. I'm intrigued to see how you've taken to—"

The conversation was halted by a knock on the door, and, suddenly, she wanted more time. Strange how that worked, but the realization that the vial was missing, likely taken by the one person she knew would recognize it, made new questions form in her head. Alice announced herself just as she had before. "I have brought the Captain of the Guard, his soldier, and the young Lord Renald with me," she added. "I'm coming in."

When the door was opened, Alice was the first one in, but the Captain was not far behind. If it wasn't for his unwavering courtesy, Alice might have been knocked out of the way. Relief washed over him the moment he saw her standing there. "Oh, thank the stars," he breathed. "When I woke, I was so worried. Veroh said you were fine, but I didn't want to believe it until I saw it with my own eyes."

"Yes, I'm fine," she said. In a manner of speaking, anyways. She gave the Doctor a faint nod. "If you would, lead the way. And you're right. We should have a little talk once this is all settled with the Queen."

The journey through the twisting halls of the airship was a quiet one, full of tension and unasked questions. The

Doctor attempted to spark a conversation with the group about their various wounds, how they were feeling and how they were taking to their treatments. The Slayer was silent through most of it, listening carefully for suggestions of any questionable actions on the part of the Doctor, but he seemed to have tended to them as anyone would and she hopefully had nothing to worry about.

Finally, they reached a set of ornate doors with etched wood and gleaming copper arabesques twisting over them to resemble wild vines and roses. Two men stood flanking the door, standing prim and tall with long, bladed weapons. Several more soldiers stood ready in the shadows, nearly blending in with the posts that held the ceiling up. They eyed the group with mild suspicion, especially the sword hanging from the Slayer's belt.

The Doctor took the lead, bobbing his head and smiling at the guards. "I know the Queen isn't expecting her new guests for a little while now," he said, "but it seems they were quite eager to meet with her. Might we be permitted inside?"

Exchanging a slightly dubious look, the guards considered this, then one nodded to the other. The other seemed to hesitate, but he nodded back. Without a word, he reached over to pull open the door, his comrade following suite. The Doctor led them in to a bright room, contrasting sharply with the darkness of the ship's halls and inner chambers. As wide as the massive ship itself, the room stretched from one window-lined wall to the other, large windows that revealed the blue sky and misty clouds passing by. Each wall was concaved slightly, making room for balconies looking over the world on each side. It was clear that most of the Queen's court held their audience here, the crowd as varied and lively as a village green during a celebration feast. A few eyes drifted to the small party curiously, but they drifted back to their business soon enough, sipping wines, nibbling fruits, lounging on couches or reading books. It was surreal to think that the world toiled under the threat of Soulless while they relished in luxury overhead, gained from their travels and the Queen's prestige. The Slayer forced herself to look past them and their excess, reminding her of Paravelle, to the back of the room, where a half circle of cushioned benches were situated on a raised dais. At the center of the handful of delegates sitting there, observing and chatting amongst themselves, was, at last, the Queen.

She noticed the Slayer's entrance immediately, lifting a brow and keeping the corner of her eye on her progress across the room. The others sitting beside the Queen were less subtle with their looks, but the Slayer kept her attention on the figure at the center of them all. Though she was getting on in her years, she wore her age as well as she wore her glittering jewels and her fur-lined satin. She had the presence of some graceful bird, with her long neck and her noble, aquiline nose. Her auburn hair, streaked heavily with grey, was swept back behind her in a regal bun, delicately decorated with a copper band of a crown that placed a sparkling emerald at the middle of her forehead, an emerald that brought out the green in her sharp hazel eyes. She leaned forward in intrigue, sparing a smile for the comment whispered in her ear by the dark-skinned woman to her right, who eyed the group up and down a moment before snapping a black lace fan out to cover the lower half of her face. Only her dark eyes were left to be seen, shining eagerly like an animal on the prowl, a look that reminded the Slayer far too much of the Baroness.

"And so the Savior of the Untouched graces my fine ship once more," said the Queen, her voice warm with a gentle smile to match. "It has been a while, my dear, and I can only imagine you darken my doorway with troubling news once again. As much as it joys me to see you, I know you never bring good tidings."

"Never good at all," the Slayer agreed. Beside her, her companions and the Doctor dropped down to their knee, ducking their heads in respect, but the Slayer remained standing. "Your Majesty, we come from Paravelle to inform you that something has gone terribly wrong there. The Baroness has released a swarm of Soulless on the city in the night. We barely escaped with our lives, and odds are that the city is completely overrun with them now. We came to warn you, and to let you know, and to seek your council on what should be done."

The Queen straightened, brows knitting as her pleasantries fell. Excited and confused whispers rippled through her court, filling the room like the very murmur of the engines down below. The Queen lifted a hand to quiet them. "This is...startling news, to be sure. We were planning on visiting Paravelle after we met with the Duke of the City on the Lake. Are you certain it was the Baroness?"

"Positive," the Slayer said. "I saw her instructing them myself. That's another thing, Your Majesty. Not only had the Baroness been keeping all the dead of her kingdom in a pit to grow and thrive as Soulless, but she had somehow managed to control them."

She wanted to say more, to mention the little vial that she had found and that it had gone missing, but, behind her, she heard the Doctor draw in a sharp breath, holding it. Better evidence that he had taken the vial she couldn't imagine, outside of finding it on his person right then, but it was also a clear sign that he knew something about it. A dark feeling crept under her skin, and she held her tongue, just as she had with Lord Gizak. She would follow Veroh in this, to gather more information before acting brashly.

The Queen's brow seemed to twitch; was that a telling sign? The Slayer hoped that Veroh was paying attention, since she was far better at these unspoken clues than she was. "Control them?" she asked. "How is that even possible? The Soulless have no sentience of their own. They listen to nothing but the most carnal desires and needs."

"Yes," the Slayer said, "I know, but I also know what I saw. They were listening to her. They had somehow gained a sort of sentience, and that is why I had to come to you, so that you could know. The Doctor has more knowledge of how those creatures work than anyone else. Perhaps he can figure out how, and stop it before it becomes a new epidemic. It's one thing to control the scourge when they are just mindless corpses; it's something else entirely if they should start to think for themselves."

If it weren't for the steady, constant thumping of the engines and the propellers of the ship, the silence in the chamber would be deafening, as the meaning of these words started to weight on everyone's shoulders.   For a brief moment, the Slayer felt some loathing for the crowd gathered in this room, perhaps worse than the blind sheep of Paravelle, floating above the world and barely acknowledging it. But the Queen shifted on her seat, her face shifting through expressions as she shifted through thoughts, clearly disturbed and eager to help. The Slayer contemplated mentioning the missing vail, but this was not the time. She would have to seek a private audience with the Queen, away from the Doctor, perhaps even the others, as well.

"This truly is dire news," the Queen finally managed, but she nodded resolutely. "Our solution, for now, is clear. Let us finish our business here at the City on the Lake, and then immediately set course for Paravelle. Slayer of the Soulless, I trust you will help us plan to get back to the fortress and get a closer look at this epidemic ourselves."

While the thought of returning to that death trap and the cesspool it had likely become sent a chill racing through the Slayer, she nodded.   What other proposal had she expected? She knew all along they would be returning to Paravelle, but at least now she had the Queen and her arsenal at her side. "Of course," she said. "It won't be easy, but I'll do whatever I you need to get to the bottom of this. Which, if I may be so bold, your Majesty, I believe might require a more private audience. Perhaps we could arrange something?"

The Queen lifted her chin, eying the Slayer with a more speculative look, but eventually, she nodded in understanding, a frown deep on her face. "Certainly. I understand. We'll have plenty of time for private matters on our way to Paravelle. For now, though, I wish to think on all of this, have some time to perhaps consider what should be done. I'll let my people down in the City know to finish up their business quickly. I'm sure we can have our course set for Paravelle by mor—"

Something loud and booming cut the Queen off, dulled by distance, but clearly coming from far below them. The troubled look of consternation returned to her face, as the room went quiet again to listen. If it hadn't been for the collective response, the Slayer might have thought she imagined it. Then she heard it again, and she realized what it was, looks of shocked recognition appearing all across the room.

"The cannons," the Queen breathed out, a hand covering her mouth. "Those are the cannons from the City on the Lake. They haven't been fired for years, why would they be firing them now?"

As a murmur of discussion rose up from the Queen's court, several people moved to the windows, to step out onto the balcony for a better view. It was just then that the Slayer noticed the small telescopes attached to the railing, where men and women leaned over to peer down at the city. Cries of alarm and confusion joined the din of speculation, several of them backing away from the telescopes with a look of horror on their faces.

"What?" the Queen demanded, rising to her feet. "What is it?"

She had her answer moments later, when breathless guards came thundering through the ornate double doors at the far side of the room. "Your Majesty!" they gasped. "The City on the Lake. It's under attack!"

CHAPTER SIXTEEN

Under attack?" Her eyes wide, the Queen stared at the soldiers rushing forward with the news. "By what? That's impossible!"

"About as impossible as an attack in Paravelle," the Slayer noted coldly. "What is it? Is it Soulless?"

She hadn't needed to ask. One look on the horrified faces of the courtiers who had peered down on the city through those telescopes was all she needed. One of the men were in the corner of the balcony, doubled over as he released his lunch.

"Y-yes," one of the soldiers stammered, his face pale and troubled. "We were down in the observation room, waiting for the group to get back with the steel supply, when we saw it happen. One minute, we were watching the people of the city go about their business, and the next minute, there they were. They came out of nowhere! Those people down there don't stand a chance!"

His words inspired another wave of murmurs, distressed and concerned. "Move aside," said the Queen, striding toward the balcony with purpose as she nudged anyone who wouldn't clear a path out of her way. "I must have a closer look."

The Slayer wasn't going to wait for an invitation. She twitched her head to signal to the others to follow, then made her way to the balcony to claim her own telescope as well. She took grim satisfaction in the fact that people seemed just as eager to clear out of her way as they had the Queen. She took far less satisfaction in the view that awaited them over the railing and down far below.

One didn't need a telescope to see that smoke was already billowing up from various sections of the City on the Lake, proving that all areas of the large island were under duress. Another cannon boomed loudly, and the faint sound of screaming rose up with the wind. The Slayer quickly took a cold telescope into her hand, leaning forward to peer in and swivel the instrument around for a good look.

She saw the edge of the lake first, the ring of Soulless kept back by the water, but still reaching over the waves toward the thick stone walls. There was no threat there, nothing shocking, unless one considered that the thick ring made it impossible for anyone to escape. The carnage beyond the water and beyond the walls only made their hunger greater, and there were so many of them that the Slayer swore she could hear their moans. Feeling her throat tighten, her mouth gone dry, she refocused her telescope, back over the wall, into the destruction of the city, where the true terror was.

"It's happening again," she muttered to herself. "It's happening here, too."

Far below, well beyond their reach, the City on the Lake resembled a carcass burst open from the inside; the Soulless were like the frenzied, feeding maggots crawling all over it. Through the gaps in the roofs and buildings, she could see Soulless swarming into the courtyards and streets, overtaking the screaming, unsuspecting citizens. Plagued from the inside, the walls meant to protect them turned into the walls that would trap them, just like in Paravelle. The Slayer stepped back, trying to understand what she was witnessing, trying to figure out why.

Veroh was beside her, also peering down into the carnage, with the strangest look on her face. Fear and disgust were there, to be sure, but, underneath it all, there was a strange sort of understanding and determination. "What do you think happened?" she asked. "Do you think it's the same as Paravelle?"

"Somehow, someone who had been bitten must have gotten inside," the Queen postulated. "They became infected, started infecting the others, and no one realized it."

"No," the Slayer said. "There's too many of them. There's no way so many could be infected and no one realized it unless it's just like in Paravelle. Where the infected were being held somewhere else, like that pit, under everyone's noses. Believe me, when someone is bit, they don't just turn in an instant. Even the dead take time to rise again."

"What action do you want us to take, your Majesty?" The Queen's soldiers clutched their weapons as though primed and ready, though they nearly shook where they stood. The Slayer couldn't blame them, not really. They had probably dropped down to help suffering villages before, but they probably never saw anything like what waited for them in the city, especially if she was feeling a little daunted. So many Soulless, released on so many helpless souls.

The Queen stood still and stiff, her slender hands gripping the railing of the ship as her eyes seemed to pierce down into the massacre below. Another cannon went off, but it was the last one they heard. The Slayer could practically see the gears in the Queen's brain turning, just like the gears that kept this ship afloat, and, finally, the Queen closed her eyes for a moment, gathering her strength. "Follow me," she said, turning away from the balcony and sweeping past the Slayer with her graceful steps. The soldiers fell into line behind her, and the Slayer joined the ranks as she left the room and climbed the ladder down into the ship's twisting hallways.

With the flock of soldiers behind her, the Slayer had no chance of pushing past them in these dark halls to reach her, but, striding beside her, her face now a grim mask, was the dark-skinned woman with the fan. "What is it?" the Slayer asked her. "Where are we going?"

At first, the Slayer wasn't sure if the woman had even heard her. She just kept moving forward, following the crowd through the twists and turns. But there was a hardening there, a breath taken in deeply and held for a long moment of indecisiveness. "You'll see," she said, with a deep, rich voice that sent shivers through her. "You'll see, Slayer."

The determined Queen led them down into a large room near the clanking machines of the engines, the hiss of steam filling the air like strange music. The moist, warm air was suffocating, the noise almost unbearable. A series of contraptions were scattered about with a chaotic sense of order, and at the center of it all was a woman hidden under goggles and grease. The Engineer looked up with an astonished expression, pushing up the goggles from her eyes, revealing eyes like a bug's, bulging from their sockets.

"Y-your Majesty," she stammered, wiping oiled gloves on her thick leather apron, tripping slightly as she moved around the capsule-like contraption he'd been gutting. When she took in the escort of warriors, her eyes grew somehow even larger. "My..my goodness. What are you doing here? Er, I mean, what brings you here? That is...how can I help you, your Majesty?"

If the Queen was put off by her stammering, she didn't show it, wasting no time in the matter at hand. "The device," she said sharply. "Is it ready?"

A blank look met the inquiry, until a moment later, realization settled in, and the Engineer looked as though she might become sick. "The-the device? Of-of course it's ready. It's been ready."

"Good," the Queen said. "We need to use it. Immediately."

If the Engineer had been holding something then, she would surely have dropped it. As it was, she had only her jaw. "Im—Immediately, your Majesty?" she asked. "Er, I mean, y-yes, of course, but, but you can't be serious! You-you do know what-what this will mean, don't you?"

"Of course I know!" A flash of anger sent the Engineer cowering back slightly, but a deep breath returned the Queen to her cold, restrained disposition. "As we speak, the City on the Lake is being overtaken by Soulless. We created the Device with the hope that we would never have to use it, but thank the stars we have it all the same, for the hour of our need. Today is the day, as much as it pains me to say it. If it works, then we'll prepare another one. For Paravelle."

"P-Paravelle?" the Engineer looked to the Queen with a trembling expression of awe and fear. "What is going on?"

"Everything will be explained in good time," the Queen said, casting a sideways glance to the Slayer. She gave her a strange nod, one she couldn't quite decipher. "For now, I need you to prepare the device and unleash it on the City on the Lake below. Do you understand?"

"Y-Yes, your Majesty," the Engineer nodded. "Of course. We'll...we'll get it down to the hull straight away. You'd best not be near, in case anything should happen. Not that it will! But..but...you know, just in case. We can use the communication tubes, and then we'll...we'll...we'll let it go."

"Very good," the Queen lifted her chin. "I'll be able to watch the effect from the balconies, anyway. I'd like a few of you to help the Engineer get the device ready to drop." With a wave of her hand, the soldiers jumped at the chance to volunteer, and she turned to the crowd that had followed her. "Everyone, back to the main hall. There, we can observe and wait for the preparations to be complete."

"What is this device that she speaks of?" the Captain of the Guard of Paravelle had caught up with the Slayer, concern wrinkling his brow. As they moved back to the audience chamber, she could feel the others crowding closer, eager to have her answer their questions.

"I don't know," the Slayer admitted, feeling uneasy herself. "The Engineer is always working on the strangest things, so it could be anything. There's a brilliant mind in that frazzled head of hers, you all know that from everything she's brought to Paravelle. It must be a weapon of some sorts."

Back in the main hall, an excited murmur filled the room as the Queen's court jostled for a good spot to view the action. An excited murmur filled the room as the Queen's court shifted towards the windows for the best view. The Queen stood at the center of one of the balconies, where a soldier had opened a hatch in the floor and pulled out a long brass tube, a strange apparatus at the end. Out of respect, the crowd moved aside to let the Slayer through to stand beside the Queen, but the others were not so lucky, lost somewhere in the cluster of curious courtiers.

"What is going on?" the Slayer demanded, growing weary of asking that question.

The Queen sighed, her age showing in the forlorn expression on her face. "You would agree with me, won't you," she asked, "that even if we dropped every single one of our soldiers down there into the City on the Lake, we could still fail to vanquish all those Soulless?"

"Unfortunately, yes," the Slayer agreed. "It would be suicide."

"The only way, then," the Queen continued, "would be to attack them from above. Now, we have been testing a few new weapons, and there are always arrows and crossbows, but the ammunition it would take to destroy them all is unimaginable. Besides that, we would need some might good marksmen to effectively shoot them all from such a distance. But what if we had a weapon that could destroy them all in one fell swoop? Of course, such a thing would devastate the city it was being unleashed upon, and there would still be no guarantee it would even have destroyed the Soulless. So the device is...something the Engineer and the Doctor have been collaborating on. When it strikes the earth, it should release a chemical cloud. The Doctor believes that this chemical will effectively counteract whatever it is that makes a Soulless Soulless, and effectively stop them. Now, we haven't tested it yet, obviously, but if the City on the Lake is already gone, I can't think of a better time to experiment than now."

As the Slayer listened to the Queen's explanation, that awful thumping in her blood had started up again, making her sweat, making her breath quicken. She thought of the little red vial that had gone missing from her pouch, the thought of the blood rushing through her own veins. Of course the Doctor had been working on something to neutralize the virus, but to be able to unleash it so swiftly and completely?

"That's amazing," she managed, breathing out in hushed awe.

"If it works," the Queen added gently.

The Slayer's racing blood now seemed to tingle under hear skin as those last words resonated. If it works. If it worked, then the plight of the Soulless might once and for all be ended. If it worked, then there's be no place for her in the world any more. If it worked, she may as well have agreed to the Baroness's offer, for what else would she do? The legends always spoke of the great Slayer of the Soulless putting an end to the scourge, but this device would prove those legends wrong.

If it works.

A muffled voice emerged from the end of the brass tube in the Queen's hand, the voice of the Engineer somewhere far below them. "The device is prepared and ready for launch," she said, her voice tinny and distant, but still trembling with excitement. "Commencing countdown."

The Engineer started to count off, starting at ten and dropping down with a slow and steady pace. The measured approach to the moment of truth felt like the longest ten seconds the Slayer had ever experienced.

CHAPTER SEVENTEEN

For all the tension and held breaths in the room, the impact of the device after it whistled down to the earth after being released from the airship's hull was surprisingly anticlimactic. A deep rumble rose up from the ground, like an earthquake, and then the smoke began to billow up from where it had landed. Black at first, it seemed like a cloud of dust rising, then spreading over the city like a fog as the color started to become tinged with red. It almost reminded the Slayer of blood, the way it would mix with mud after an attack in the rain, seeping everywhere from the dead bodies.

The rumbling continued, like thunder rolling in the distance, and any of the faint traces of screams from below faded away into an eerie quietness. No one quite knew what to do in the airship floating above the spreading cloud, until someone tentatively asked, "What do we do now?"

"We wait," said the Queen, allowing a small sigh to escape her, loosening her stiff posture slightly, "for the smoke to clear. Perhaps a day or two, then we can send a group down to investigate, to look for survivors."

"A day?" the Slayer asked. "But that's so long!"

"Perhaps even more," the Doctor said. "The viral component of the device will linger for a while. It shouldn't be harmful to humans, but we can't be certain. It's never been tested on such a large scale before, and it may have adverse effects for some."

The Doctor looked at the Slayer when he said this, and she didn't like the feeling of those eyes and what they meant one bit. Almost without realizing it, her hand drifted to her arm, in the bend of her elbow, where she could swear she could feel her blood moving. She narrowed her eyes, barely hiding a scowl. What sort of madness had he created now? What had they just unleashed on the City on the Lake?

"What about Paravelle?" the Slayer asked. "It will take us time to get there. Shouldn't we be leaving soon?"

"Even more reason to wait," the Queen replied. "We'll send the Doctor and his scientists down into the city, as well, so they can have a better idea of how it worked. That way, they can use what they gained here to ensure that we can do the same in Paravelle. But, since we can do nothing but wait, we might as well get some rest before the decent. We'll send a reconnaissance team down to investigate tomorrow. I trust you would be willing, if not eager, to join this group, Slayer?"

The Slayer's eyes flitted to the Doctor, who tilted his head thoughtfully, then gave the slightest of nods. The Slayer, in turn, nodded to the Queen. "I would, yes."

"Good," the Queen smiled. "We'll get to the bottom of this together, and soon, everything will be right again in the world. Until tomorrow, though, we wait. I think I may retire myself. You are all dismissed."

The dismissal left the courtiers buzzing, milling about and eager to discuss the exciting event with each other, and the Slayer had the feeling they would remain chattering in that chamber for quite some time. The Queen departed on the arm of the dark-skinned woman, who sent a lingering gaze toward the Slayer before disappearing through a door behind the dais. Knowing she would not enjoy talking to any of these people, the Slayer considered what to do with this idle time, looking for Veroh so they could depart back to their rooms and talk in private. When she turned to look for the other woman, though, she found herself faced with the Doctor.

She had to admit feeling a little startled by his proximity, feeling that familiar rush of anger through her veins. "What do you want?" she demanded.

"To talk," he said. "But not here. Let's go to my laboratory. We'll fix you up with something to help you sleep."

He reached for her, to gently guide her by her elbow, but she jerked her arm away. "Help me sleep? I don't need—"

"Something to sleep," he cut in, speaking louder and more obtrusively, before dropping his voice to an exasperated whisper. "I swear, you have all the subtlety of a bull in a china shop. Just come to the lab. We need to talk."

Her confusion allowed him to guide her out of the chamber, but when they were alone in the hallways, she yanked herself free. The mere touch of his cold, clammy hands made her skin crawl with disgust, made her stomach twist in knots. "What is going on?" she demanded. "What is that virus you put in the device? How do you know it works? Is it going to be safe for me to go down there tomorrow, or..."

She couldn't continue; she couldn't bring herself to say the words that were marching through her brain. She felt sick, though she couldn't tell if that was the implications or just the usual feeling that seemed to course through her when she started to feel upset, when she became incredibly aware of the virus coursing through her own body, the virus that the Doctor had put there, the virus that had supposedly saved her life.

"And what did you do with that vial of red liquid?" she asked, changing her focus, hopefully moving it away from her. "Why did you take it? What is it? What do you know about the Baroness and her Soulless?"

"Just wait!" the Doctor hissed. "There are ears everywhere, even if you can't see them. My laboratory is the only truly safe place to discuss this."

The journey to the laboratory seemed to take forever, but, once they had arrived, the Doctor did not hesitate to answer the questions that were burning inside of her. "Calm down," he said, first and foremost, holding out his hands as though to settle her that way. "I can see you getting worked up, and that won't do any good. How are you feeling? Do you feel ill? Do you feel upset?"

Scowling, the Slayer tightened her fists to keep from lashing out at the man. "I did not follow you down here for a check-up, Doctor," she said. "What is going on? What did you do with that vial? What is it, and why did the Baroness have it?"

The Doctor sighed. "I do wish you'd cooperate," he said. "For science. You've taken to your antidote better than anyone else I've ever seen introduced to that strain of the virus, you know. And while I'm incredibly proud of the strain released by the device, I would love to see how I could improve on it. Just a blood sample, that's all I'll need. You're astonishingly resilient, you know."

"So the virus in the device is similar?" she asked, not letting herself be distracted.

"It's stronger," the Doctor said. "And while I had to inject you with your antidote, putting it directly into your blood to counteract the virus, this one can be breathed in, working through the body a little differently. Not to mention, your antidote was designed to attack the virus before it could take a hold of you. This one is meant to attack the virus that has already taken a hold of a person. It seeks it out and destroys it, and, unfortunately, it also destroyed the subject."

"Unfortunately," the Slayer repeated with a snarl of disgust. "Leaving you without test subjects, am I correct? And what about the vial? Why did you take it? What does it mean?"

Sighing again, the Doctor moved to his desk and sunk wearily into his chair. He looked down at the messy surface a moment before he lifted his eyes back to her. "I didn't want anyone else to find it," he said. "Simple as that."

"Because you knew what it was," she said. "It came from this very laboratory."

The Doctor nodded. "I can't deny it."

"I should kill you, right here, right now, for that. Did you know what that liquid would do? Did you know how she was planning on using it?"

"Do you know what it does?" the Doctor challenged. "Or are you just guessing? The fact of the matter is that only I know what that liquid does and what it was for. And only I have the secrets to the virus that might lead to our salvation. I'm the only one who has the cure, and yours is breaking down, isn't it? You won't kill me. You can't afford to."

The more the Doctor spoke, the more the Slayer's blood pounded in her ears, thumping through her veins hot and irritable, the harder it became to breathe. She forced her eyes closed for a moment, trying to control it, but it was becoming more difficult. He was right, of course. If she killed him, she would be destroying all the knowledge inside that bald cranium of his. She'd be killing the chance for answers, just as she had with the Baroness. But the urge for blood was strong. Her hands flexed open and closed, drifting closer to the hilt of her sword, but she could also use her bare hands, forgoing the weapon and getting right to the jugular. Then again, she didn't necessarily need to kill him. Just as long as he could talk. All she needed was blood.

She had just wrapped her hand around the hilt of her dagger, a much more efficient weapon for these close quarters, when she heard something crashing beyond the door on the far side of the laboratory. The ship had listed slightly to the side, disrupting her balance, and she heard the crashing again, followed by what she thought was a faint moan. It may have all been her imagination, a trick of her riled-up senses, but she recognized that groan, and it cut through the chaos of her body to strike fear straight to the core of her.

"What was that?" she demanded, eyes flying open.

"You're overworked," the Doctor said, placing his hands on his desk and standing up. "You need to calm down and rest. And you have to let me examine you. I study this virus, Slayer. It's my entire life's work, and I can recognize the signs of relapse when I see them. How long have you been feeling like that?"

"No," the Slayer said, pounding a fist on the desk. She thought she heard something pounding in response beyond the door. "I am not overworked. I am not relapsing. I'm fine, and I heard something behind that door. What is it, Doctor?"

"You should rest," the Doctor said. He found her eyes with his, locking them together in a gaze both pleading and stern. "Let me take a sample, please. You may be at risk. No one has ever gone as long as you have without the virus overtaking them. I have to know your secret."

"And I have to know yours," the Slayer said. "Tell me the answer to my questions, and I'll give you the answer to yours. Starting with what's behind that door."

"I can't tell you that. Not now. It's too dangerous. But I will tell you that, no, I didn't know what the red liquid you found with the Baroness would do, not entirely. It was an experimental strain of the virus, and she wanted to start running her own research. This is a lot of work for a single man, you have to understand that. I have my scientists, but still, we can only accomplish so much. The Baroness had been keeping the bodies of her dead, as you already discovered, so we had an excellent source of test subjects. I would have been foolish to say no."

"Does the Queen know about this?" the Slayer asked.

The Doctor shook his head . "You know she'd never approve."

Eyes dancing to the door at the back of the laboratory, the Slayer wondered just how many things the man was doing without the Queen's knowledge, and whether or not she should say a word. Discretion was never one of her strong suits, but she was learning that there was a time and place for everything.

"Did you know that what you had given the Baroness would allow her to somehow control the Soulless?" she asked, the conclusion sticking in her throat as she tried to express it. "That's the only explanation. Whatever is in that little red vail gave those monsters some sort of sentience. Did you know?"

The hesitation was all she needed. A low groan escaped her, unbidden, and she thought she heard a moan answer back, but it could all be in her head.

"Please," the Doctor said. "You don't understand."

"Maybe I don't," she allowed, "but I do understand this. What happened in Paravelle is in your hands now. You made this bed, and I expect you to lie in it. You will create another device. We will use it on Paravelle. And, as soon as that's complete, you will meet your justice."

She was unable to stand in that room anymore, her stomach churning, her desire to exact that justice now racing through her, a terrifying bloodlust that sawed on her nerves. It took every ounce of her consciousness to hold her back, reminding her that they would still need the loathsome doctor for a little while longer. She turned around, feeling better just to have him out of her sights, and reached for the handle of the door.

"Wait just a moment!" the Doctor called. "What about my blood sample?"

She barely paused to glance over her shoulder. "You'll have to get it from my cold dead body," she said.

"It'll hardly be much good then," the Doctor muttered, "unless you plan on coming back as a bloody Soulless."

But the Slayer shrugged her shoulders. "I can think of worse fates," she said, though she truly couldn't, the idea of being unable to control her urges as she had in that small laboratory making her feel sick. Not wanting to give the Doctor another chance to reply, she finally opened the door and stepped outside, though she had to lean against the wall to regain herself after she had closed the door. The thumping of the engines somewhere nearby made the walls hum. The clanking of gears made her wonder if she truly had heard something behind the door, or perhaps it was just the ship itself, all the strange mechanisms and hissing steam that made it run. She was losing her mind, and she almost regretted that she hadn't managed to get something to help her sleep. It would be a long time before the smoke cleared, too long to just be trapped inside a floating airship with her own thoughts.

CHAPTER EIGHTEEN

Sleep eluded the Slayer that night, unable to put her busy mind to rest with all its new information and concerns. If the occasion of slumber did happen to reach her, it was brief, ended by some vivid nightmare, all of her worries brought to life inside her head. In those brief flashes of dreams, she let the virus finally overtake her, turning her skin green with decay, making her limbs weak, muscle peeling off from the bone. Words failed her, coming out only as desperate moans while she reached for Veroh, pulled her close as she fought, then biting into the tender flesh of her neck as her screams rang through the nightmare. And then there were the dreams where the Doctor, wielding a long syringe like a sword, laughing as he plunged the needle into the Queen and ordered her to attack. Illogically, the Baroness was there, too, turned into a Soulless as well, and the two women descended on her to consume her and tear her apart. And then there was the City on the Lake. Though the airship still waited overhead, the Slayer stood at the center of the city, and all was quiet, all was still. There were no people, there were no Soulless. Only her, all alone, and useless.

"Is everything alright?" Veroh asked, once morning had arrived and they sat eating a meagre breakfast before going to join the others in the audience chamber. "You look as though you haven't slept a wink."

The Slayer gave a noncommittal grunt in response, stuffing her mouth with bread. She supposed she could open up to Veroh, explain everything to her, perhaps even find some sympathy from the other woman, but the Slayer just wanted to focus on the day at hand, to get down into the City on the Lake, and then move on to Paravelle. Besides, in light of the Doctor's underhanded dealings with the Baroness, she wasn't feeling particularly trusting. Thankfully, Veroh seemed to be feeling accepting, as she didn't push the issue, though the wrinkle of concern made frequent appearances on her brow.

When they reached the Queen's chamber, Kyle, Renald, and the Captain of the Guard were already there, standing in a cluster and trying to ignore the eyes on them from the morning courtiers. "Any sign of the Queen yet?" the Slayer asked them, also brushing past the lingering glances. "Or perhaps her general? I believe he is going to be leading the expedition down to the city?"

As if on cue, the Queen appeared through the door behind her raised dais, her companion and her general in tow, the latter appearing ready for anything in newly shined armor. "Ah, excellent," the Queen nodded as she took in the Slayer's small group. "You're here, which means we've only just to wait for the Doctor and his assistants before we send you down to see the device's work for yourselves. Are you all planning to go?"

"I am," the Captain of the Guard said, stepping forward with a hand to his chest. "As is Kyle. Veroh, I believe you should stay here."

Veroh seemed startled by this news, blinking with surprise and opening her mouth to protest. But her quick wit seemed to be at play here, as she then settled back and reconsidered, then gave a grave nod. "You're right," she said, "I'll stay. With Renald. This may be a good time to inspect the Queen's library, don't you think?"

While Veroh might have been surprised to be excused from the excursion, Renald appeared to be relieved. "Yes," he said, meeting Veroh's gentle smile. "It will be."

As they waited, they did a brief check of equipment, the Queen's General offering to outfit them with a few more daggers and crossbows, which just made the Slayer wonder why weapons were such a concern if the device had truly done its job. The Doctor arrived and handed out a new supply, thin paper masks on strings, meant to cover their face and nose in case anything in the air might still be toxic.

"I thought you said that the virus was safe for humans," the Slayer challenged, eying her mask with distrust. "Why would we even need these?"

The Doctor's eyes lingered on her for a bit too long, making her feel as though the masks were not so much for the benefit of the group, but for her in particular. "Better safe than sorry," he said.

A cursory examination from the telescopes on the side of the ship showed that the vile mist had faded and the City on the Lake was settled below them in complete, eerie stillness. Down below in the hull of the ship, they prepared for the long decent, equipped with harnesses and hooks to help them. The wind was roaring in their ears, whipping about anything that wasn't held into place, and they had to shout out instructions as lined up by the thick rope ladders.

"Would you like the honors?" The Queen's General shouted, gesturing toward the ladder. The Slayer eyed him cautiously, weighing his sincerity and searching for signs of a trap. She found none, only patience, perhaps a little nervousness, and she nodded. She took the rope, and began the long, harrowing decent through the hatch into the wild open world.

Grateful for the fact that heights had never bothered her, the Slayer held on tightly as the wind pushed the ladder, making it sway, but the more bodies that descended down with her, the more they weight seemed to stead it. The City on the Lake seemed so far away and small, and it seemed impossible that she could ever reach it. She kept her eyes forward, though, focusing on the steady climbing, on moving, down, down, down, until her feet miraculously touched the tiled roof of one of the city's towers.

The Captain of the Guard was next, followed by the General and his soldiers, the Doctor and his assistants, one after the other, and she was there to help them regain their footing. The Slayer glanced around, looking for weak spots in defense or wandering enemies, but the device's aftermath left the place feelings like a ruin, a city of the dead, nothing but the wind, much gentler down here closer to the ground. All that remained was an emptiness that she had only seen after the most devastating of battles, and, even then, there were always a few stragglers. The City on the Lake was devastated, bodies lying below in the streets, still and motionless. A chill started at the base of the Slayer's spine and moved its way slowly up, until she had to shake slightly to dislodge the ice from her nerves.

"Incredible," the Queen's General breathed out in awe. He released the grip on his weapon, easing into a comfortable stance. "I guess the device lived up to its promises."

"Guess so," the Slayer echoed, but she was not so quick to relax. Enough time had passed so that, if the device hadn't neutralized the virus, then those bodies down below would have gotten up again, new Soulless created from dead humans. It was hard to tell from the tower which of them had actually been humans and which were the Soulless that had been crawling over the city. She peered over the side of the tower, then dropped down to the top of the curtain wall, where she nearly landed on top of two bodies, one dressed in the armor of a guard, the other with clear signs of decay. The device must have hit just as the Soulless was about to bite into the soldier, both of their mouths open, one in eager anticipation, the other in a silent scream

"I thought you said the device was harmless for humans," the Slayer said, frowning down at the bodies, nudging them with her foot. Her sword was out and ready, and she swiftly sliced off both their heads, stomping their skulls, the crunching sound seeming to echo in the stillness of the city.

The Doctor winced, having just joined her after some help from the others. "Please don't do that," he said. "You're destroying very good specimens there. I hope to lift some of them back up for a closer look in my lab. And you're right, it shouldn't have any adverse effects on humans. This poor fellow must have been bit, so the virus was already working through him."

Wondering if anyone else would notice that it was clear the soldier had been unharmed, the Slayer addressed the more direct issue. "What if the device didn't work, or only delayed the inevitable? I would rather we didn't get attacked if I can help it."

"Just leave them be," the Doctor said. "They're harmless now, and I need them for my research."

Not far away, there were more soldiers and Soulless corpses alike, and, as the others gained their bearings, the Slayer moved forward to inspect them closer. Kneeling beside a soldier, she wrenched off his helmet, inspecting the glassy eyes that looked up vacantly into the sky. The Soulless nearby was nearly on top of him, and she moved him around, this way and that, looking for signs of a bite or even a scratch. Nothing on the neck, one of the Soulless' favorite spots, but, wait, no, there, at his side. He wore a mere breastplate, with nothing to protect his back, and there she found a festering wound. Her jaw tightened as she stayed her hand, fighting off the natural habit to take her dagger and shove it into his face. Was she really to trust that the device had worked?

She couldn't just leave it. She stood a moment to get her sword, which then cleaved through the corpse's shoulder to slice off his arms. She did the same to his legs at the kneecaps, and, when she moved back down to slice off his jaw, the Doctor had noticed.

"What are you doing?" the Doctor cried out. He gawked helplessly at her as she moved to the next one to do the same. "Have some respect for the dead! You're ruining potential subjects that may help us!"

Scoffing at the Doctor's idea of respect, the Slayer cleaned her blade before fixing him with a steady glance. "I'm taking a precaution," she said. "You can still do whatever you'd like in your research, but now, if he does turn, then at least he can't hurt us. If they've been bitten, they could turn at any moment."

"But the device!" the Doctor insisted. "If it worked, it would have neutralized the virus."

"And if it didn't," the Slayer replied, "then we're about to be in a lot of trouble. Better safe than sorry."

"So, we're going to just lob off the limbs of everybody we come across?" the Queen's General scoffed faintly. "That will make quick work of our exploration."

The Slayer fixed him with an unappreciative glare. "We do what we must. Come on. We won't find much up here. We'll have to go deeper into the city to really get a good look at how the device has worked."

"Should we split up?" the Captain of the Guard asked. "We could cover more ground that way."

"I think it's best we stick together, else we'll be likely to lose each other entirely," the Slayer mused, after considering both options. "Either way, we should get down to ground level. Odds are, that's where most of the action took place."

She started to move toward the tower, where they could find a stairway to take them further into the action, but she felt a hand fall lightly on her arm. "Wait." It was Kyle, his brows knotted in a look of confusion. "I thought I saw something, over there."

He pointed, through a gap in the rooftops and walls where a small courtyard could be seen. The Slayer narrowed her eyes, leaning forward slightly. How anyone could have seen anything that far away was beyond her, and, since it was Kyle, she felt slightly inclined to believe him paranoid. She shook her head. "I don't see anything."

"Something was moving," he said. "I thought it was just my imagination at first, a trick of the shadows or maybe a banner in the wind, but, no, it wasn't like that."

"I don't see—" But just as the words were leaving her mouth, something shuffled into her field of vision, too far away to tell much detail, though it was certainly the size and shape of a body. She gasped in surprise, her heart leaping into her throat, as the figure shuffled into their field of vision, then out of it again.

Her gasp had caught the attention of the others, so she and Kyle weren't the only ones to witness it. "A survivor!" the Queen's General proclaimed. "It worked, and we weren't too late. Quickly, let's find our way to that courtyard so that we may help them."

"Wait," the Slayer said, to stop the flow of eager soldiers toward the stairs. "The way that body moved wasn't human. If there are survivors down there, I don't think they'll be the kind of survivors we want to find."

"Are you saying it's Soulless?" one of the Doctor's assistants tentatively asked. "But the device should have destroyed them all!"

"Maybe your device didn't work as well as you had anticipated," the Slayer said darkly. "Come on. We'll head down to that courtyard and get a closer look. If there are survivors, we can help them back to the ship. But I can recognize a Soulless from a mile away. That thing didn't move like a survivor; it moved like the undead.

"We should probably send one group in," she continued, while the others gawked at her, dazed and shellshocked. " Have the others remain here," the Slayer suggested. "No point in all of us waltzing into a massacre."

"A potential massacre," the Doctor corrected testily. "We know nothing for sure, but you're right, we shouldn't take chances. I'll go, and the General, and I'm sure you'll want to go, too, Slayer."

She nodded, then turned with a silent question to the Captain of the Guard. "I should stay here," he said. "Just in case. We shouldn't group all our strongest warriors together."

"Agreed," the Queen's General nodded stiffly.

The Slayer turned, to give directions to the Captain of the Guard in case something should happen, when she noticed something in the shadows, behind the small cluster of the Queen's soldiers and the Doctor's assistants. One of them was standing further back, near the roof of the tower where they landed, by the dark doorway that would lead them down to the courtyard. Everyone was present and accounted for, but she could see someone else, an additional figure, moving around inside the shadows of that room beyond. Her stomach turned in realization, and she reached for her sword, rushing forward without sparing another moment in hesitation. Hesitation could mean death.

She was too late, though. As soon as she moved, the figure in the shadows revealed itself, encouraged by her movement, a grey-faced Soulless growling as it reached for the nearest prey. The Doctor's assistant screamed, and, like a rabbit caught in a trap, her squirming attempts to escape only tightened the Soulless's snare on her. The creature sunk its teeth into the tender flesh of her shoulder, thick blood welling up to stain the whiteness of her shirt. A gnarled hand scratched down her back, tearing her open, and she went limp in its grasp.

Both scientist and Soulless fell to the ground in an awkward heap, the latter ceaselessly gnawing away as she screamed in pain. The Slayer hissed nervously, afraid the screams would attract more Soulless, but Kyle surprised her, proving to be quick and efficient lobbing off the creature's head and smartly stabbing through its skull. Face to the floor, the scientist breathed heavily through her sobs, still overwhelmed despite no longer being attacked. She would suffer no further, though, as Kyle swiftly drove his blade into her head as well.

"What are you doing?" the Doctor shouted, grabbing Kyle's shoulders and pulling him away from the corpses as he breathed heavily, trying to catch his breath, a small fleck of grey matter on his cheek. "We could have saved her, you fool! You've murdered her! You imbecile!"

Kyle attempted to shove himself free from the Doctor, but the man, his round face red with rage, held tight, clutching his armor and shaking him. "Get off me!" Kyle snarled. "Did you see what that thing did to her? Even if she did survive, she was bitten! It was hopeless!"

Realizing that Kyle didn't know about the antidote that the Doctor had developed, a dark shadow passed over his face and he let Kyle go, albeit roughly. "You don't understand," he said. "You just don't understand. If I have created a virus to counteract the Soulless, what makes you think I haven't created something to cure it before it sets in?"

"Obviously, you haven't counteracted it," Kyle said, finally wiping his cheek as he pushed himself up to his feet. He gestured angrily at the Soulless corpse. "What was this? If your device was effective, this shouldn't be here!"

The Doctor remained on the stone floor, shaking his head. The Slayer watched him carefully, and the interesting array of emotions dancing across his face. "Maybe...maybe it was protected, by the inside of the tower. Perhaps up here was too far for it to reach. Somehow, it wasn't exposed to the release of the virus. Somehow, it just..."

"We're going down there," the Slayer decided, reaching her hand out to the Doctor to help him up, if only so he could see the anger in her eyes. She felt him trembling when she took his hand and pulled him to his feet. "Those of you staying here, I want you to climb back up on that roof, signal to the airship to be ready to leave at a moment's notice. If it's just a few stragglers, we should be fine, but if the device didn't work, we have a big problem on our hands."

Her directions were met with grim agreement, though it was decided that the Doctor should say, putting his trust in his assistants, no doubt to save his own hide. The Slayer couldn't focus on that right now, though. With the small exploration party set and ready to go, they wasted no time to let their nerves get the best of them. They drew their weapons and marched dutifully for the tower, uncertain of what might await them beyond.

Chapter Nineteen

As she lead the slow march down the twisting tower stairs, the Slayer started to wonder if that attack on the scientist had been part of some collective imagination run rampant, some strange, shared lucid dream. Everything was so still and quiet, their breathing magnified by the empty space and the darkness. Even at the next few landings, the opening into the hallways held nothing but shadows dancing from sputtering torches and dead bodies sprawled out ravished but unmoving. "Just in case," she murmured, as she instructed the soldiers to crush the skulls or stab their brains. Some of them hesitated, but the cold reminder of their friend's fate strengthened their resolve.

Halfway down, they found the body of a dead soldier, sprawled across the stairs, reaching for a sword nearby, though not nearly close enough. He was on his stomach, the hard leather of his studded jerkin peeled back like the skin off a fruit to reveal the torn up mess that was his back. Soulless had carved him open, digging inside for all the best, soft organs they could find. There they stopped, though, having left the thick, meaty muscles of his limbs. They hadn't bothered to remove his helmet, either, to get to his tender brains, the ultimate treat, so soft and flavorful. It seemed like such a waste, the Slayer thought, licking the corner of her dry lips. Kyle was already kneeling beside the man, grunting slightly as he turned him over onto his back. Again, they were met with those glassy, dead eyes staring back at them. The soldier's mouth was open in a silent scream, and it would likely be moving again, growling and moaning like the same thing that killed him.

"Poor son of a bitch," Kyle murmured, flicking the gore from his dagger after he took care of the potential threat. The man's eye had wedged itself onto his blade, and he grimaces as he pulled it off. It fell to the stone floor with an odd plop, and he idly stepped on it, squishing it underneath his foot.

"Show some respect," one of the Queen's soldiers wrinkled her nose distastefully. "It's the least we can do. That man fought to the very last, like a true hero."

"The last thing we need is some recently turned Soulless grabbing at our ankles as we pass it by," Kyle growled back. "If he died fighting to the last, imagine how he'll be when he comes back."

"Be quiet," the Slayer hissed, when she thought she heard something as they neared the bottom of the tower at last. "Both of you. The last thing we actually need is an ambush of Soulless just because two idiots couldn't keep their mouths shut."

This seemed to quell them both, for a moment, and a hush settled over them as they all listened for those awful moans, the relentless shuffling, or even the slopping sound of a feeding Soulless, something, anything, to give them an indication of what waited for them through the door to the courtyard. The Slayer narrowed her eyes, trying to determine whether that soft brushing was a moving creature or just the gentle breeze. "It's strange, though, isn't it?" Kyle said, his trembling voice a whisper. "Where are all the other bodies? At Paravelle, there were whole mountains of them, but here, there's barely any. And they're not eating any of the brains, it's almost as if they're leaving them to—"

Putting up her hand, the Slayer stopped the flow of his speculation. Not only did they need to be quiet, but it would do them no good dwelling on the implications of this strange Soulless behavior. She put a finger to her lips to emphasize the silence as she slowly crept down the last few steps, edging toward the door way. The others followed close behind her, the tension between them thick and electric.

"Well," said the woman who had previously argued with Kyle, "here are all your bodies."

Scattered throughout the courtyard, in various states of disarray and dismemberment, corpses covered the cobblestones like carpet, and, among them, the Soulless were still feeding, digging and tearing and trying to find just one more good piece of meat, one more tasty organ, among the already savaged and decaying bodies. Some of them fought against themselves, nudging into each other and seizing each other eagerly before realizing that they were no prize. The

Slayer's stomach twisted, realizing how much time had passed and how desperate these Soulless much be if they were picking through dead bodies as old as these. Soulless didn't want dead meat, they wanted fresh meat, living flesh and sinew, juicy and flush with pumping blood.

And they were all fresh meat, just standing there, arriving at the scene like a feast to the starving masses. The gentle breeze pushed their scent across the courtyard, but, even without the wind to help, they would have realized it soon enough. The nearest Soulless, down on its knees in front of a hollow-faced woman who seemed little more than bones any more, was the first lift its head, the gaunt muscles stretched over its skull twitching strangely as it picked up the aroma. Turning its head to see the group standing there, it released a rattling groan, excitement and hunger all in one. It dropped the woman's emaciated arm and crawled up to his feet, staggering forward with reaching arms.

The Slayer braced herself, waiting for the Soulless to be close enough that it pierced its chest on the tip of her sword and still kept walking forward. The weapon dug deeper, and she leaned back, out of the reach of those gnarled fingers, the yellowed claws scratching at the air. The other Soulless were paying attention now, too, slowly stalking over to take what the first one would did not consume.

With the Soulless moving around as much as it did in an effort to reach her, the sword now creeping through him and out the other side, the Slayer was surprised to find that she couldn't hold him there and reach her dagger at the same time, a common trick, so she could stab it into the Soulless' face before it got her. Grunting with effort, her brain wildly spun for a potential plan, but the Soulless suddenly went limp, the weight of its body nearly bringing her sword crashing down to the ground. Protruding from deep between his eyes was the butt end of a crossbow bolt, and the Slayer turned her head to see Kyle standing there, up a few of the steps, with a crooked grin on his face and his bow hefted up on his shoulders.

"Good thing I've done all that target practice," he murmured.

"And you're about to get a lot more," the Slayer said, pressing a foot down on the Soulless corpse and yanking her sword out just in time to send it slicing down through another one. "Get ready! Here they come!"

"Keep back!" the Queen's General shouted, directing their small army. "Let the entrance work as a bottleneck so we don't get overwhelmed! Get your bows ready!"

She couldn't have said it better herself. As she and one of the Queen's soldiers stood guard at the door, Kyle and another kept their ground a few steps up, bolts and arrows whizzing by them to find a home in the Soulless' skulls. Eventually, though, the bodies began to pile up, effectively blocking the way, and the Slayer backed up. "We climb," she said, jerking her head for the stairs. "After so long without fresh meat, they're not going to let a wall of corpses stop them. I think it's time we went back."

The others were not about to argue with her, though a scream cut through the air, as the archer beside Kyle tumbled down the stairs, knocked over by a Soulless who clung to him tightly and clawed at his chest. Kyle had just enough time to shoot a bolt into the Soulless' back before he, too, had to fend with another, using his bow like a shield to block it as it snarled and snapped.

"We've got trouble!" he called out.

"How is that even possible?" the Queen's General turned to see the struggling soldiers with his eyes wide in surprise. "We took care of all the corpses we could find!"

"Clearly, we didn't find them all," the Slayer said, but she wasted no time in discussing what they could not change. Already, the press of the Soulless outside was causing a body or two to fall from the blockade, so she hurried forward to assist Kyle with his attacker. "There's no time. We have to plow through them and get back to the top of the tower as quickly as we can. Move!"

The stampede was panicked and hurried, every shift in the shadows making them leap, and thank the stars, because most of them were Soulless that just seemed to appear right from the woodwork. The Slayer's heart raced as she cleaved a path through the creatures like clearing away foliage through a thick forest. They didn't have time to ensure that they didn't get up again, they didn't have time for anything except climbing those stairs wildly, grateful for the fact that, no matter how many Soulless appeared, at least the humans were quicker and could maneuver going up stairs better.

When they reached the top of the stairs, the bright sky above was a welcome sight, as was the excited call of the group that waited for them. They were already in the process of lifting one of the dead soldier's bodies up into the airship on a long plank; the Slayer's heart leapt into her throat, but it was too late now. At least she'd dismembered the corpse so that it couldn't do much more than moan and writhe in a little bit.

She could already hear the question coming out of the Captain of the Guard's mouth, so she anticipated it as she helped the others up onto the roof. "No time to explain!" she shouted. "We have to get back up on that airship now!"

As she shouted up, a voice drifted down, halfway up the rope where the dead body swayed in the wind. "He's turning!" cried the voice of one of the scientists with the corpse. "What do we do?"

"Do nothing!" the Doctor shouted back up, a grin blossoming on his face. "We'll have a live specimen! So to speak."

"Slayer!" Kyle shouted down at her, reaching his hand out, and she realized that she had been gawking up at the Doctor with revulsion and horror. To think that he would willingly bring a Soulless onto the ship, no matter how incapacitated, made her wonder if he hadn't done something like that before. There was a hard not in her stomach, thinking of all the things that could go wrong if, for whatever reason, things went awry. "Come on!"

The moans of the Soulless coming up the stairs echoed in the shaft of the tower, seeming even more haunting and spine-tingling. Battling with the strange mess of emotions roiling inside of her, the Slayer knew she could do nothing about it now. She could only grab Kyle's hand and let him help her up to the roof, where they would be safe from the reach of the Soulless that had come after them. Ropes started to unfurl from the opened hatch at the bottom of the ship, just as the Soulless started to appear and mill around under the lip of the roof, where they stood watching them out of their roof.

Kyle shot a few more bolts into the growing crowd, but the Slayer set a hand on his arm, shaking her head. "No point in wasting ammo," she said. "There's nothing we can do now."

"There's nothing we can do yet," the Captain corrected, giving her a concerned, worried look before taking a hold of one of the ropes and starting to climb back up into the sky.

CHAPTER TWENTY

Back in the Queen's airship, in the small, private room behind the dais in the larger audience chamber, the Slayer, the Doctor, and the Queen's General stood before her to bring her the disturbing news. The three of them stood as still and stiff as they could while she paced back and forth in front of them, mulling over the information. "What do you mean, they were still alive?" The Queen, in all her confused fury, made for an impressive, almost terrifying sight as she turned on them. "How is that even possible?"

"The device didn't work," the Slayer said, after it became clear that the Doctor and the Queen's General were not being forthcoming with the information. In her peripheral vision, she thought she saw the Queen reach for her heart, a small sound escaping her. "Not on the Soulless, anyway, or at least not in the way the Doctor expected. It was...strange. It appeared to work only temporarily, if I could fathom a guess. When we saw the city, it was dormant beneath us, but once we ventured in, once there were fresh, warm bodies nearby, they woke up, as if from a slumber."

"But I've seen the tests," the Queen said, stopping now in front of the Doctor and piercing him with a gaze that he tried to avoid. "They were inconclusive when we did them in the laboratory. The virus counteracted whatever made the Soulless Soulless and killed them once and for all, as effectively as a stab straight to their brain. What was it? Was it not powerful enough?"

"That...that is a possibility," the Doctor managed, finally lifting his eyes toward the Queen, though they didn't stay for long, dropping to the floor as he explained. "Perhaps it was the nature of the device. It wasn't able to disperse a strong enough dose of the virus, and, instead of ceasing their animation all together, it merely suspended it for a while. There are so many factors at play here that aren't an issue in the laboratory. The fresh air, something in the release mechanism, even the wind itself could have all played a factor in its ineffectiveness."

"Oh, yes," said the Queen. "All the factors, except the one where perhaps your product was faulty?"

The rebuke seemed to hit the Doctor like a physical blow, causing him to flinch as the color drained from his face. It surged back, though, red and bright with fury over the insult. "M y product is fine," he choked. "It worked perfectly before. There is some other factor at play, something I had not accounted for."

"Perhaps we need to consider one thing," the Slayer said. She was no fan of the Doctor, especially considering what she knew of his recent dealings, but getting to the bottom of this was far more important than personal feelings. She did pass a cool, judgmental glance his way, though, watching him squirm as he no doubt feared she may spill some of his secrets. "Perhaps we're not dealing with the same sort of Soulless we're used to. What are the odds that this would have anything to do with what happened in Paravelle? How would those Soulless have gotten into the City on the Lake in the first place? Wasn't the Baroness's sister brought to the City on the Lake to wed the Duke here? Could she have been collecting dead bodies in a pit below the castle, too, waiting for the right moment to release them?"

"Why now, though?" the Queen asked. "Why not wait until after we had left?"

"Maybe they were trying to send a message," the Slayer said.

"Maybe they knew we would investigate. Maybe they knew was on board and thought perhaps I would go down to fight them. The Baroness released her Soulless to kill me, we're all convinced of that. Maybe the Duchess did the same, in attempt to lure me."

"I suppose the one thing they didn't expect was the device, though," the Queen murmured, as though she was speaking out loud to get some of the racing thoughts out of her head. It didn't seem to work, though, as she shook her head, massaging it with her fingers, and went to have a seat in a tall-backed chair facing the three of them. "It makes no sense! None of this makes any sense!"

Unsure of what to say, the small audience remained quiet, everyone in the room mulling over these conflicted thoughts and details. The Queen's eyes snapped up suddenly, though, as a thought seemed to appear to her. Those steely daggers dug deeper into the Doctor. "You have that body, though," she said. "Of one of the soldiers. You can examine him, perhaps figure out exactly what is different about those Soulless and the ones you've been experimenting on so far."

"It's possible," the Doctor said. "He hasn't turned yet, but, yes, it's possible. If there are any differences, I can use that to improve the virus for a new device, one to unleash on Paravelle."

The Slayer couldn't help wondering if he already knew the differences, if the secret was held in that little red vial. But there was deep concern knotting the Doctor's brow, a disturbed contemplation that made her wonder what he was thinking, and if she would really want to know.

"Let's get to work, then," the Queen said with a sigh, signs of her age creeping into the lines of her face. She looked so weary and tired, and, for a brief moment, the Slayer saw in her loose skin a glimpse of a Soulless. She shook her head to clear it of the bizarre thought, but it made her realize just how exhausted she was, too. "Doctor, I want you to get started on a stronger strain immediately, especially if you can use the soldier you brought back to figure out if the Soulless are getting stronger or if it was some other things that prevented the device from working. We'll set our course for Paravelle immediately, and pray to the stars that we can find some sort of answer there. You are all dismissed; I need time to think about this matter."

The Doctor excused himself amid bobs of his head and apologies; the Queen's General was also prepared to leave until he realized that the Slayer stood still. The Queen regarded her with a questioning lift of her eyebrow, and she explained. "I'd like to have a word with you, Your Majesty." Her eyes flicked toward the soldier. "Alone."

Hand to his hilt, the Queen's General stiffened, a look of warning going to the Queen. But, with a tired wave of her hand and a soft sigh, she dismissed him again. "It's alright," she said. "Leave us. If she decides to dispose of you when your back is turned, at least she can't get very far, and then someone else can deal with this mess."

The General hesitated a moment longer, then nodded his head stiffly. "I won't be far," he said, slipping out the door.

"You're far too trusting, Your Majesty," the Slayer said, after waiting a moment, though she figured the Queen's General was still right outside the chamber door. "Which is precisely what I wanted to speak to you about. Do you think we can truly trust the Doctor?"

The wan smile that the Queen offered almost seemed to suggest that she had known this question was coming. "I trust him as much as I trust you," she said, "or anyone for that matter."

"But is that wise?" the Slayer pressed, suddenly wishing she had Veroh at her side, who would be able to guide her on what she should say and what to hold back. She wanted to shout out that the Doctor was deceiving her, wanted to bang her fists on the table and demand that justice be served, though the Queen's blessing be damned, she would likely do it anyway. But she knew that they needed him, as the Queen softly echoed, as if she had read the Slayer's mind.

"We need him," the Queen said. "Just as we need you."

The Slayer winced to be grouped in the same category as that man, but the Queen's quiet, pleading eyes digging into her softened the blow slightly. "How much do you know?" the Slayer asked, ll

But the Queen just smiled softly, sadly, and leaned her head back against the headrest of her chair. "I know that I'm tired," she said. "I know that it feels as if we've been fighting an endless battle our entire lives. I don't know exactly what we'll find in Paravelle, but I do know that we will find something. All of this will eventually end, that much I know, though I don't know exactly when. I look forward to it; I hope I'm there to experience it, though it seems so far away that I very much doubt that I will."

She's hiding something, the Slayer thought. We're all hiding something.

"Is that enough?" she asked.

"That, I don't know," the Queen said. "But we'll find out soon."

To Be Continued in

The Slayer Saga:

HEARTLESS

August 2015

ACKNOWLEDGEMENTS

I owe a great deal of gratitude toward everyone who helped to make this book possible, almost too numerous to count, though I will make an attempt to thank those in particular who made this book possible. I had two incredible beta readers, Jody Moller and Denise D. Young, who helped change my perspective on certain aspects of the story and made it stronger because of it. If I'd have given myself more time, I could have implemented more of their ideas, but I hope they find the final product improved from their input.

When I discovered her via Design Cuts and solicited her for a potential cover, I couldn't have ever dreamed that Ingrid Pomery would produce such a stunning visual for the book. She was wonderful to work with and, through the graphics provided by Kirsi Iggy Rouvinen and Laura Davison, she has created a truly unique and spectacular cover for my book, one that will easily set it apart from what else is out there in the world. I cannot wait to work with her more to develop the next two covers for the series.

Another big help in producing this book was my first venture into Kickstarter, which allowed me to gain fourteen marvelous "backers" to help contribute to the financial costs of producing this book. Little by little, their small contributions added up to a great big help, and you can read more about them down below.

Finally, I'd like to thank all the people who supported me throughout the process, encouraging me and inspiring me to strive on. These are family, friends, colleagues, anyone who would bother listening to me babble or rant for more than five seconds. I just hope this book met your expectations, and, if not, well, I know you'll be there to encourage me through the next endeavor, and they're only going to get better from here on in.

CONTRIBUTORS

One of most exciting aspects of this book was that it happened to be the first time I tapped into a crowdfunding source like Kickstarter to help raise funds to make publication possible. The response was incredibly uplifting for someone who really had no idea what she was doing. I'd like to offer a special thanks to all the people who contributed to the campaign; you were a bit help, and, as promised, I'd like to share with you all a little bit about these wonderful people. If you enjoyed this book and look forward to the next volumes, please take the time to visit and support those who helped to make it possible.

So a few shout-outs go to my wonderful backers: Daniel W. Butler, Rob Crosby, Cryolite, Emilie Ferre, Amber Genzink, Michael Grip, Alexander Kimball, Matthew Lowe, Antonio Rodriguez, Michelle Scharmack, Kate Sparkes, Alejando Torres, and Scott

Weiffenbach (aka Bomfan, Cubs fan, gamer, streamer, and supporter of this Saga).

You can follow Ken Johnson on Twitter @panzeryelp

Kate Sparkes would like to welcome you to Darmid, where magic is a sin and fairy tales are contraband via her book, Bound, (YA Fantasy). Available now in paperback and e-book.

And a few other things from my contributers:

"Remember to always smile!"--Michelle

"Qapla!"--Emilie

"May your heart always lead you to the compassionate choices."--Matthew

"I do not have a book yet. How ya'll doing?—Alex

I cannot thank these generous contributors enough for their faith in *The Slayer Saga*, and I hope they are not disappointed in what they finally find resting in their hands.

Special Excerpt:

Bound

(Bound Trilogy Book One)

by Kate Sparkes

An excerpt from Kate Sparkes'

Bound

Available now on Amazon.com

in print and digital copy

Chapter One

Aren

The barmaid didn't offer her name to me as she would have to any other unfamiliar man who entered the tavern, but it was there at the front of her mind. Florence, though she preferred to be called Peggy. I could have dug deeper into her thoughts and memories to find out why, but it didn't matter. She didn't matter. She was just another loose end I was going to have to tie up at the end of the night, another irritation in a long chain of them.

The wooden clock on the wall read half-past eleven as I moved toward a table in a dark corner, trying not to draw the attention of the half-dozen border guards who were preparing to leave. I wished only to be left alone, to get the information I needed and move on. The hood of my cloak blocked my peripheral vision, but I kept it up to cover the shoulder-length hair that would identify my status as an outsider in this strange land.

A red-haired brute bumped my shoulder as he slipped into his heavy coat, and he cursed at me. His friends laughed. They'd have been more cautious if they'd understood what I was.

For the sake of my mission, I allowed them to leave unharmed.

Peggy knew what I was. Every time she glanced in my direction, her thoughts jumped to the preserved dragon head in the back room. She pushed the thoughts away, refusing to make the connection. It was an attitude I was familiar with. The people in this country, Darmid, feared magic. They'd spent centuries destroying every form of it within their borders, protecting themselves from a threat they didn't understand.

Few things irritated me more than willful ignorance. I needed to get home to Tyrea before I snapped and strangled one of these people who so reminded me of spooked cattle.

The barmaid ignored me as the seconds and minutes ticked audibly by on the intricate monstrosity mounted behind the bar. Her anxiety grew, pushing out of her in high, fluttering waves that I ignored. I breathed slowly and deeply, focusing my magic on the area outside of the inn, staying aware. All was quiet. Peggy and I were alone.

She jumped as a tiny door on the clock popped open and a bright red bird popped out, tweeting an off-key tune that did nothing to lighten the atmosphere. It pulled her out of her anxious stupor, and she turned to me.

"Drink?" she squeaked.

I shook my head, and she went back to sharing her attention between the door and the clock.

"We're closing soon," she said a few minutes later. "Do you…" she hesitated, torn between emotion and professionalism. "Do you need a room?"

"No. Only a few more minutes, and I'll be on my way."

She nodded, but made no move to begin closing up.

The door flew open, blown back by a gust of wind and rain. A slender man entered, wearing a black coat matching those of the men who had left earlier. He struggled to pull the door shut behind him. The hat he wore low over his eyes had done little to keep his face dry, and his thick mustache dripped rainwater down the front of his already-soaked garments.

He nodded to the barmaid and removed his hat as he passed. "The usual," he muttered.

He turned his head from side to side as though sniffing for danger, paused as he caught sight of me, then hesitated for a moment before sliding onto the bench across the table from me.

I took a moment to reach outside of the building again with my mind. He had followed my instructions, and had come alone.

Drops of water from the hem of his coat made dull tapping noises as they hit the grimy floor, out of time with the clock. He knocked his fingers on the table and pretended he wasn't afraid, but his thoughts pressed out of him, propelled by uncontrolled emotion. Fear, dread, a touch of excitement. Seeing a person so exposed repulsed me, and once again I longed for this assignment to be finished.

So finish it, I thought.

"You are Jude Winnick?" I asked him, dropping my voice to a pitch and volume that grabbed his attention but left the barmaid unable to listen in.

She interrupted us, leaving the safety of her post long enough to deposit a cup of sharp-scented spirits in front of my companion. She ignored the droplets that sprayed the table as she retreated.

He drank deeply, then wiped his mustache on the sleeve of his coat. "I am."

"Your brother is Myles Winnick, the magic hunter?"

"Might be. Might not be." His words were confident, but his voice trembled. "I know who you are, Aren Tiernal. I know who *your* brother is. I could turn you in."

Half-brother. Even as I worked to gain Severn's favor, I couldn't help but distance myself from him in my mind. "Is that why you answered my message, why you came here tonight? Are you going to place me under arrest?" I allowed myself a small, humorless smile and leaned forward, catching his gaze with my own. "No one knows you're here."

He licked his lips and took another long drink, then signaled to the barmaid to bring more. She looked away.

Winnick cleared his throat. "What do you want?"

"Your brother has been a busy man lately."

Winnick snorted. "Well, he's good at what he does. He sniffs out people like you better than a fox after rats."

"I'm looking for a magic-user born in your country. Any one would do, but your brother is killing them off. It's inconvenient."

"Not for us, it isn't."

"It could be."

Another attempt to drain the dregs from his cup, and a scowl. "Why don't you talk to Myles about it? He's the magic hunter. I'm just the muscle."

I leaned back and rested my hands on the table. "Your brother is well-protected, and I don't think he'd be interested in speaking to me. But you—you could get close to him. Pass on a message. I heard a rumor that he's captured another Sorcerer. Perhaps he'd be interested in letting me take that person with me. Far less messy for your people than trying and executing him."

The drink must have been strong. Winnick's inhibitions were lessening after just one serving, his confidence growing. He pushed the cup too far to the side of the table, and it clattered to the floor. "And help you Tyreans? Not bloody likely. Why do you want him for, anyway? As I hear it, your country's just lousy with people like you. What do you want with ours?"

"That's not your concern." *Nor is it mine*, I added to myself. My brother Severn, regent of Tyrea, had ordered me to bring him a magic-user from Darmid, and to make sure no one in our own country saw me do it. I didn't care what happened to them after delivery. I just wanted to find one so I could leave this magic-barren land behind and return home for a reprieve from the manipulation and the killing.

I wasn't eager to see Severn again, but some things couldn't be avoided.

Winnick grinned, revealing several gaps in his yellow teeth. "What if I told you we'd just executed that one this morning? That he died bitching and moaning about his innocence, how he couldn't help having magic?"

I clenched my hands into fists under the table, but held my temper in check even as my pulse quickened. "I would be displeased if I heard that. Is your brother tracking anyone else right now?"

"I don't know."

But he did know. Had I not been able to read his thoughts with magic, the shift in his eyes and the nervous twitch of his wrist would have given him away.

"Look at me." He obeyed, and in an instant I was past his almost non-existent defenses, probing his thoughts. "Where?" He felt me in his mind, and tried to push the name of the town away, but I caught it. *Widow's Well.*

"How uplifting," I whispered as I released him. He collapsed back against the booth and tried to pull his thoughts together. "You're a monster," he gasped.

"I wouldn't have to be if you'd cooperate."

"I'll never help you." He shuddered, then pushed his short hair back from his brow. "My brother will hear of this, and his superiors, and theirs."

"I'm terrified." I glanced at the barmaid. She stood straight and still, jaw clenched as she listened, looking anywhere but at us. At least her ignorance and fear were working in my favor.

"Are we done?" he asked. His right hand slipped under the table.

"Don't." I spoke sharply enough that the barmaid risked a glance in our direction. "This won't end well for you if you attack me."

He didn't listen. The hunting knife gleamed dully in the lamplight as he raised it and held it tight in his trembling fist. I gritted my teeth. *I should have taken that drink.*

Winnick stood and adjusted his grip on the knife's bone handle. "I don't think you mean for this to end well for me either way. I know about you people, and where your power comes from." He blinked and looked around. "I shouldn't have come. Making a deal with the bloody devil himself, that's what this was."

I stood, reached slowly into my pocket and produced a heavy gold coin, which I set on the table. "So you're not interested in a reward for the information you've so generously shared?"

His eyes widened, and he swallowed hard. His left hand reached for the coin, but he pulled back. In that moment of unguarded distraction I forced my way deep into his mind, past thoughts, memories and desires. He tried to close himself off, but it was too late.

I had all of the information I was going to get from him. I decided I would alter his memory and let him go. After all, Severn wanted this done quietly. I could be done with Winnick in a matter of moments and go on to search elsewhere for a magic-user.

Memories flooded Winnick's mind. Images of people he had helped his brother hunt down. Men, mostly, and hardly any with significant power. A few might have been classed as Sorcerers if they'd had the education and opportunity required to develop their talents, but not one had been given the chance. I saw them hanged. I saw a young woman screaming as the hunter and his men dragged her away from her crying children as her neighbors looked on and did nothing. And I saw this man and his brother laughing over their victories in this very tavern. My breath caught in my throat as rage finally overtook me.

Winnick bared his teeth in a mad grin. "You see that?" he whispered.

He tried to back away. I didn't let him, and his eyes widened as he understood the extent of my control over him. His knife clattered to the floor, though he tried to hold onto it. His thoughts turned to pleading, his emotions to fear and desperation as he tried to anticipate how I would hurt him.

A low moan escaped his throat, and behind him the barmaid clapped both hands over her mouth. I ignored her. She wouldn't remember any of this once I was through with her, and neither would Winnick. Not until he had to. Not until the suggestion I planted in his mind was ready to become action.

To hell with subtlety.

I leaned closer, and whispered to him what he was going to do.

Made in the USA
Lexington, KY
16 August 2014